THE GIRL WHO COULD NOT DREAM

Sarah Beth Durst

CLARION BOOKS ★ HOUGHTON MIFFLIN HARCOURT ★ BOSTON NEW YORK

CLARION BOOKS
215 Park Avenue South
New York, New York 10003

Clarion Books is an imprint of Houghton Mifflin Harcourt Publishing Company.

www.hmhco.com

The text was set in Sabon LT Std.
Title page illustration by Andrea Femerstrand
Hand-lettering by Leah Palmer Preiss
Book design by Sharismar Rodriguez

Library of Congress Cataloging-in-Publication Data
Durst, Sarah Beth.
The girl who could not dream / by Sarah Beth Durst.
pages cm
Summary: Sophie's parents run a secret shop where dreams are bought and
sold. When Sophie dreams, her dreams become real, so she is forbidden to
have any. Sinister events are set in motion when she is accidentally seen by
one of her parents' customers, and it's up to Sophie to save her family.
—Provided by publisher.
ISBN 978-0-544-46497-1 (hardback)
[1. Dreams–Fiction. 2. Families–Fiction.] I. Title.
PZ7.D93436Gi 2015
[Fic]–dc23
2015001324

Manufactured in the United States of America
DOC 10 9 8 7 6 5 4 3
4500574949

1
IMAGINARY LOCKS

THE LOCKS WE USE TODAY WERE INVENTED BY A GUY named Linus Yale in 1848, but his son, Linus Yale Jr., made a way improved version in 1861. He was like, *Great invention, Dad, but I know how to make it better,* and that's exactly what he did, and then his dad was like, *Awesome, thanks.*

History is full of cool facts like that. Real life, not so much.

The awesome thing about historical facts is that they're really easy to learn. You can get them from school, obviously, but also from books or the Internet or TV, and there's no end. You can learn as many facts as you can cram into your brain. Then, when your mom says things to you at night like "stay in bed" even though you're twelve and it's a weird thing to say, in your head, you can be like, *Alaska was purchased from Russia in 1867*, and it almost drowns her voice right out. And when she pulls your tie-dye covers all the way up to your neck, and you look really close at her eyes and realize there are tears in them, you can roll away from her and think, *Iceland has the world's oldest democracy.*

And when she says, "I love you, Sophie"—well, that part is okay to listen to, because that's a fact, even if she has a funny way of showing it.

I rolled back around so I was facing her. "Love you, too," I said.

Another fact. I really did love her, but after almost four months, this bedtime routine was getting a little old. And depressing. Definitely depressing. Like the kind of depressing where the teachers who promise never to give homework on the weekends give homework on the weekends. But since it was mostly my fault she was like this in the first place, I just had to deal with it for as long as it went on.

She closed my door and made a clicking sound with her throat, which was supposed to be the imaginary lock she put on it so I couldn't get out.

Imaginary locks were invented in 2017 by Molly Mulvaney, aka Mom.

She put the same kind of lock on the front door to our condo, not when we went *out out*, like to school or grocery shopping or any of the other regular life things we still did, but usually just at night, and usually just for her. Nights were when she got the saddest, when she wanted to go downstairs to the second floor the most and knock on Pratik's apartment door, even though she knew that would be a super awkward, bad thing to do, probably even worse than the time I called Demarius Gilbert last year in fifth grade on New Year's Eve and told him I liked him.

So she pretended she was locked in, and I was locked in with her.

And that was fine with me, mostly. I didn't have anywhere to go. It was late enough that my best friends, Kaya and Rafael, were probably in bed, too, and it wasn't like we could go out for pancakes or anything. So when Mom put the imaginary lock on my door, I left it there, and I didn't go downstairs to Pratik's apartment (because we both knew that's what she *really* meant by "stay in bed"), and she didn't, either, and maybe my not going downstairs somehow helped *her* not go downstairs, and maybe that was a good thing. I definitely owed her a good thing or two.

But maybe, I was starting to think, it wasn't so good at all.

What was so wrong about seeing Pratik? He and Mom had gone out for almost two years, so he was practically family and we missed him a lot, even though they broke up four months ago, not long after school started. Just because he and Mom weren't together anymore didn't mean we had to be "stay in bed" about it.

Maybe if I could figure out how to help her, this weird bedtime ritual could end. I pulled back the covers and sat up straight. The problem was, there was only one person I knew who could help me figure Mom out, and that person was Pratik.

I got out of bed.

Maybe Mom's imaginary lock invention wasn't perfect. Maybe, like Linus Yale Sr., she needed her kid to make a few improvements.

Maybe imaginary locks were meant to hold firm only sometimes.

Other times, maybe they were better off broken.

2

DOWNSTAIRS

I THREW ON MY BATHROBE AND CAREFULLY TURNED MY
doorknob. If my imaginary lock had been a real lock, it
would have probably made some weird clicky noise,
totally waking up Mom and getting me in a ton of
trouble.

I peeked around the corner to make sure Mom's
door was closed, tiptoed out of my room, and inched
toward the front door.

Part of me expected some scary loud alarm to go off
as I grabbed my key and opened the door. But I went
out into the hall and nothing happened except for my
stomach feeling as twisty as the garlic knots Mom and
I had eaten with our pizza for dinner.

Mom used to call us the Adventurous Girls. We used
to *be* the Adventurous Girls before and during the time

she dated Pratik. It used to be a no-brainer to order the hottest, spiciest garlic knots on the menu. It used to be a no-brainer to do any of the fun, adventurous things we did: getting off the bus at random stops and exploring new neighborhoods, taking flying trapeze lessons by the lake, trying every different ride at the state fair, even the really fast ones and the upside-down ones and the ones that flung you into freezing cold water . . . but all of that was before. Now we had to try to talk ourselves into doing stuff like that, but we didn't try that hard. Mom would be like, "You want to?" and I'd shrug and be like, "Do you?" and she'd shake her head and we'd go back to watching our movie on TV or whatever and that would be it.

The truth was, we only had garlic knots tonight because there was some deal where they came with the pizza for free. I only ate one. Mom only had a bite. We threw the rest away.

I paused before I took the final two steps to get to the second floor. This was where Mom and I used to stop for our typical Stairway Selfie. We'd smile and snap a shot or two or ten with one of our phones, just to make sure our hair was good, nothing weird was hanging from either of our noses, and we were both still looking as cute as we had when we'd left our place.

After all, it was at least a twenty-second walk from our condo to his. A lot could change in twenty seconds. I knew that better than anybody.

Twenty seconds was all it took for me to ruin Mom's life the first time.

And another twenty seconds to ruin it a second time with Pratik.

But maybe a third twenty seconds could fix it.

The garlic knot in my stomach felt bigger and knottier as I reached Pratik's door. I needed to be brave for Mom. This was not even a scary thing I was facing. This was a door.

I brought my knuckles to the wood, tapping twice, softly, and then stood back and waited, but no one answered. I glanced down at my Minnie Mouse slippers. What was I expecting, anyway? That Pratik would open the door, see me, and magically remember how much he cared about us and how much fun we had together? That he would come upstairs so Mom could be happy again?

When the Revolutionary War was going on and the colonists lost their first few battles to the British, they were pretty bummed out. They started thinking maybe all those rules and taxes and stuff wouldn't have been so bad after all. They felt totally silly. And standing in the hallway with no one but Minnie Mouse to keep me company, that's how I felt, too—maybe Mom invented the lock rule for a reason.

After waiting for what seemed like a thousand years (or at least until ten-thirtyish, which I knew it was because if I'm still awake at ten-thirtyish at night, my eyelids get droopy and my cheeks feel weirdly sore), I decided to do the only other thing I could think of: go outside. Pratik didn't always answer his door, but he usually left his shades wide open.

I crept down the stairs to the first floor (Ms. Wolfson's floor), and then opened the door that led outside. I pulled my fuzzy blue bathrobe closer to my skin. Chicago winters seriously don't mess around. Maybe a coat would have been a good idea. But I wouldn't be out for long. Just long enough to see if he was home and maybe figure out a way to get him to answer his door.

I hurried to the giant tree in front of our building and hid behind it. Then I slowly peered out, my droopy eyelids in full swing, and forced those droopers up. Pratik's light was on. He was totally home. I knew it.

He was sitting at his table, holding a fork and eating something that looked pretty fantastic. That was one of the awful things about Pratik—he was an incredible cook. Well, now it was awful, since we didn't get any of the food anymore. Even now, in the middle of the night, just thinking about his amazing spicy curry and naan and tandoori chicken made my mouth water up a storm. Oooh, and his spaghetti with the fancy turkey meatballs. And his chicken enchiladas. And his—

Okay, I had to focus.

The rest of the neighborhood was eerily quiet. Even on a Tuesday night in February, there was usually something going on in Wicker Park. Our condo was right off Milwaukee Avenue, where all the restaurants and stores were. But tonight, I could only hear the rustle of the wind. *Go back inside, you weirdo,* it seemed to say. This was a bad idea.

So I took one last look at Pratik and glanced toward the front door, figuring out how I could run back in without him seeing me or tripping and falling on my face. But maybe it would be good if he saw me. I guess I had the same problem Mom did when it came to Pratik—sometimes I wanted to see him and be seen, and other times I would do *anything* to make sure I was hidden away. It was usually one or the other, and whatever the feeling was, it was always really, really strong.

I tugged on the strings of my bathrobe so it wouldn't come loose and fall off during my attempt at a sprint, and then I peeked up one final time. *I'm down here, Pratik. I'm down here, whatever yummy-looking greenish-tannish thing of deliciousness you're eating without Mom and me.*

Poor Mom. She would probably love a greenish-tannish thing of deliciousness right about now. And she couldn't have one.

Pratik didn't look out the window. But wait—what was that? I scrunched up my eyebrows and tried to see closer. There was some sort of whitish bubbly thing hanging over him, like a funny-looking hat that wasn't actually attached to his head.

I tilted my head to the side. It had to be at least ten forty-five by now; I was probably losing my mind a little bit. This was super-duper-droopy-eyelid/weirdly-sore-cheek territory.

But was I really losing it? The thing definitely looked like a bubble, like the kind you see in cartoons with the three little dots coming out of the character's head leading to a big bubble where you can see their most private thought, the thing they're really thinking but can't (or won't) say out loud.

The big bubble, I was 99 percent sure of it now, was hanging over Pratik's head like it was no big deal. And, even freakier, there were words inside it, slowly appearing one by one. Words!

I squinted my eyes to read them.

Man, this food is amazing. I'm such a good cook! I wish Molly and Sophie were here to try this.

Just as soon as I read the words, they disappeared. What. The. Holy. Chocolate. Pancakes.

I froze to the ground, my eyes suddenly wide open and not droopy at all, as I tried to make sense out of what I had seen. The bubble was still there, but the words had disappeared after I read them. Maybe I had actually fallen asleep an hour ago and this was some sort of crazy dream. Maybe that spicy garlic knot had done something besides set my mouth on fire. Maybe . . . I didn't know.

But I knew for sure that this going-outside—going-*downstairs*—business had been a terrible idea. Now, with these freaky bubbles, things were even *more* confusing.

At the same time—he missed us! He really missed us!

I snuck back into the building, took the elevator up, opened the apartment door, slipped into my room, threw my bathrobe on the floor, and dove into bed, pulling the covers all the way up to my neck the way they were before, the way they should have stayed before I got my crazy idea and was rightfully punished for it with more craziness. I shouldn't have done that. I should have stayed right here. Why couldn't I do anything right? I'd messed up so much stuff for Mom. The least I could do was listen to her when she said to stay in bed, and I couldn't even manage that.

After what felt like forever, my heart slowed down, my eyes closed, and I convinced myself that there was no way I could have actually seen what I thought I saw. There was no way. Cartoon people had thought bubbles hanging over their heads. Real people didn't.

Unless . . . unless, somehow, they did.

3

FOUR MONTHS OF MOURNING

A MAN NAMED WALTER WASHINGTON WILLIAMS WAS THE last reported veteran of the Civil War. He lived till he was 117 years old, and when he died, Dwight Eisenhower, the president at the time, declared that it would be a national day of mourning, which meant that everyone would sit around being really sad the whole entire day.

I wasn't there, but I bet it was kinda like the day Mom and Pratik broke up.

It seemed like a normal day at first. No one was 117 years old and famous and on the verge of death or anything, so that was good. Mom was making pancakes. Pratik was on the couch, doing a crossword puzzle.

"Seven-letter word for *delight*," he said.

"Pancake," I said. He laughed.

"Not even a little bit, but thanks."

"Chocolate pancake?"

"That's sixteen letters." He smiled and threw a pillow at me.

Mom realized we were out of eggs. Pratik didn't have any either, so she went downstairs to see if she could borrow some from Ms. Wolfson. Ms. Wolfson was super helpful; she was always there to give us eggs if we needed them, and she was there if we needed anything else, too. Before Mom started going out with Pratik, I slept over at her condo sometimes if Mom got really busy with work on a school night. Ms. Wolfson made me the best cocoa I ever had and taught me how to play this really fun card game called cribbage. Besides Pratik, she was pretty much the best.

Pratik's phone rang right as Mom went out.

He glanced at who was calling and turned to me. "Can you give me some privacy, Sophie?"

"Uh, sure." I pretended to go to my room, but really, I ducked behind the couch. Adventurous Girls would never pass up a chance to have an adventurous spying session. It wasn't really spying, though. Technically I *was* giving him privacy; there was a whole couch between us. And what could he possibly need to talk about that he couldn't talk about in front of his almost-daughter?

"Hey," Pratik said in this super excited kind of voice. "Oh, I definitely got it, man." He pumped his fist in the air. "Yeah, found out last week. I can't believe how great this is." He paused. "Yeah, they have overseas offices all over the place."

Forgetting I was supposed to be hiding, I popped up and leaned forward so far that I almost fell over the top of the couch. "Overseas? Like, across seas? Like somewhere else that isn't here?"

Pratik almost dropped the phone. He shot me a look. "Gotta run," he said to whomever he was talking to. "I'll text you later."

I went back around to the front of the couch and sat down as he finished the call. Then he gave me another look.

"I know that wasn't total privacy," I blurted out. "Sorry! But you're going to go overseas? Like, to other countries? When? Where? Why?"

Pratik sighed and sat down next to me.

"Look, that was just something I shared with my buddy, okay? It's not going to be a ton of traveling . . . but it is going to be a great new job." He got a dreamy look in his eyes that was pretty similar to the way my eyes looked when I thought about pancakes.

"I haven't mentioned this to your mom yet," he added. "Think you can keep it to yourself until I do?"

I sat up straighter on the couch. It was totally my fault for listening in, but I couldn't keep a secret from Mom. Especially one like this that felt sorta big, even though I didn't know exactly why.

"Yeah, your secret's safe with me," I lied. "I'm going to the bathroom."

Ms. Wolfson's bathroom, I added silently. Seriously, didn't he know me at all? An Adventurous Girl could never keep something like that to herself. An Adventurous Girl chose the adventure. So I jumped off the couch, hopped out the door, found Mom on the stairs, and told her what I'd heard.

That afternoon, Mom and Pratik broke up. It wasn't about the new job, Mom told me. It was about the fight they got into while talking about it, and then *he* broke up with *her.*

That night, Mom changed. The national day of mourning started.

Four months later, it was still going.

A lot of me knew that the breakup was because of Pratik. He was the one who wanted to go hang out in those offices overseas, whatever that even meant.

But maybe if I hadn't told Mom, he would have decided not to take the dumb job, and she never would've known, and they never would've gotten in a fight, and they never would've broken up, and Pratik would still do crosswords and make pancakes with us every Sunday morning, and everybody would still be happy.

That's history's only problem. You can come up with all the what-ifs in the world, but you can't change anything. That's why it's history—it's in the past, it's already happened, it's over, there's nothing you can do. It was too late. They were done. The three of us were done, too. I wouldn't get to help with puzzles anymore, or eat really amazing home-cooked things, or hang out with the funniest, nicest guy I knew.

But maybe I could fix things, somehow. Maybe that crazy bubble, whatever the heck it was, could help.

After all, if Walter Washington Williams could live to be 117, I, Sophie Elizabeth Mulvaney, could fix what I had ruined: my mom's life.

4
RISK

IT WAS ALMOST IMPOSSIBLE TO CONCENTRATE AT SCHOOL the day after I'd seen Pratik's bubble, which was too bad because we were studying the Boston Tea Party in social studies and it was super interesting. Maybe I could have concentrated better if it were the Boston Pancake Party instead. I guess it would depend on what toppings they used. I was very picky. Patrick Henry once said, "Give me liberty or give me death!" For me, it was more like "Give me banana chocolate pancakes or give me waffles!" Now there's a line to put in a history book.

Kaya glanced at me from her desk on my right and raised her eyebrows as if to say *What gives?* I'd been yawning all class and she knew that was unusual. Of my friends, I was the morning person, Kaya was the night owl, and Rafael was hyper no matter what time of day it was.

I raised my eyebrows back in an I'll-tell-you-later kind of way and stuck my nose into the article in front of me, pretending like I was following along with whatever Mr. Alvarado was reading. Really, though, my brain wouldn't stop racing. I was dying to tell Mom about the bubble, but first I had to make certain it had actually happened.

I wasn't quite sure how I was going to do that.

"Now." Mr. Alvarado looked at all of us with a very-serious-teacher face. "Think about the historical figures and events we've been studying lately. Though they're all different, they have something major in common. Ordinary people—men, women, children of all ages—took risks. They did things they didn't know how to do and things they had never done before, and they did it without knowing how any of it would turn out. They were likely very scared, but they took the risks anyway to do what was right, to do what needed to be done in order to make their lives and the lives of those around them better."

I exchanged a look with Kaya. Sure, this was something different and interesting, but we both knew it was probably leading to a big, fat pile of homework.

Viv Carlson was looking at Kaya, too, and at me,

with a smile on her face as fake as her big square glasses. Those things practically screamed *I am just here for decoration, not actual seeing*. I bet if Mom told her everyone was getting imaginary locks for their doors, she'd have a hundred of them by the next day.

"Your assignment," said Mr. Alvarado, and everybody groaned, "is to think about a risk you'd like to take. It doesn't necessarily have to correct an injustice, like the Boston Tea Party—though there are still plenty of injustices to choose from in our world—but it does need to be an act that you can do that scares you a little bit. You can work alone or with partners or in groups, with anyone from this class or the class I teach after lunch, as long as each person on your team agrees that your project would be risky for everyone involved. We'll talk over more of the details next week, but for now, just start thinking. And this probably goes without saying, but let's not do anything dangerous or illegal, *comprende*?"

After class, Kaya and I met Rafael at our usual spot in the hallway. It was the exact middle point from all of our lockers, and we knew this for a fact because Kaya had actually calculated the number of feet between our lockers and done the math, determining that if we met in this spot and only this spot, we would each have the same amount of time to get to our respective lockers and then have enough time to catch up on everything that had happened since we'd seen each other last.

"What gives?" She said it out loud this time as Rafael approached from the stairs. He skip-galloped toward us, his favorite of all the weird ways to move he made up when he was bored. We called this one the *skallop*, not to be confused with the scallop that's a fish and tastes like slime.

"I just couldn't sleep," I said, and at the same time Kaya turned to Rafael and said, "Sophie is yawning," like such a crazy thing had never happened before in the whole history of the world. (In fact, I was sure lots of people yawned throughout history. I didn't have the official names and places, but it was practically a guarantee.)

"Whoa, it's eight forty-five, what gives?" he said.

"It's nothing," I said. And maybe it *was* nothing. Or maybe it was the biggest secret ever of all time. Either way, I decided, it wasn't anyone's business besides mine and Mom's.

"Ooookay," Kaya said. "So what should we do for the risk project?" It was obvious that Kaya, Rafael, and I would work together. She twisted a strand of her long black hair around her finger. Just saying the word *risk* freaked her out, I knew. Kaya was afraid of a lot of things. Except math. She loved math. She'd keep math as a pet if she could.

"Huh?" Rafael looked confused. He didn't have social studies until after lunch.

"Mr. Alvarado wants us to take a risk and do a special project about it," I said in a big, dramatic voice. "Just like all those historical people. You know, like the ones who drank all the tea."

"Right," said Rafael with a smile. "Yeah, those guys. Totally. Is it a group project? Can the three of us do it together?"

I grinned. "You know it!"

Kaya and I walked, and Rafael skalloped, in the same direction as the warning bell rang. I had English next. Rafael and Kaya had science together, and our rooms were across the hall from each other.

A crowd was gathered around Shavonna's locker (with Viv Carlson in the very front, of course), and a bunch of people were jumping up and down.

"I don't know what's happening here, but I like it," said Rafael, and he started jumping, too.

"My bracelet is stuck on top of the lockers," Shavonna told us, pointing. "Lora was throwing it to me and totally missed."

I glanced up. Our lockers were stacked in columns of three and the tippy top one went up extra high. The people who had those usually ended up sharing with a friend instead of using them because they were so hard to reach.

Rafael stopped jumping for a second. He glanced up at the bracelet. And then he looked at me.

"Sophie, do you want to try to get it?" he asked, in the same kind of voice that moms use (or in my case, used to use) when they want you to do something you don't really want to do.

"Um," I said. I could feel the tops of my ears turning red. Sure, when I was an Adventurous Girl I used to do stuff like this all the time and would've come up with ten different ways to get that bracelet before Rafael had started jumping. But now, all I really wanted to do was go far, far away.

"I could give you a boost," he said.

"Or we could go to class," I said.

"Or I could give you a boost." He grinned, and I couldn't stop myself from smiling a little, too.

He *could* give me a boost . . . I didn't really have to do anything except let him lift me up so I could reach for the thing.

"Fine."

Before I could change my mind, he dropped his stuff on the ground and stretched out his arms dramatically. We turned so we were facing the lockers, and he grabbed my waist like we had done this a million times before. It actually did work pretty well. Since he was tall and skinny—like a breadstick, only human—and I was basically a twelve-year-old trapped in an eight-year-old's short little body, he lifted me up really easily.

It had been a while since I'd done anything like this. It wasn't fun anymore. I wanted to get down.

Except before I could ask Rafael to lower me, he made a funny grunting noise and lifted me even higher.

I looked down and realized how far off the ground I was, and my heart started to thump like crazy in my chest. *What if Rafael drops me?*

"Come on, Soph," he said. "You're almost there! Show that bracelet who's boss."

I looked straight ahead then. It really was right there. All I had to do was reach just a little bit, then a little more—and—"Got it!"

The group cheered as Rafael lowered me to the ground and I placed the bracelet in Shavonna's open hands.

"Wow, you're good," she said. "Thanks!"

"No problem."

I didn't tell her that even though I was on the ground now, away from heights and bracelets and adventures, my heart kept thumping like crazy, and when I told it to relax, it didn't listen at all.

I had been in lots of high places before, places way

higher than the tops of the lockers. I'd been on the tops of trees. Rooftops. Roller coasters. That sky-tower place downtown where you sit on the glass floor about a zillion feet above the ground.

And I had been fine. Everything had been fine.

But that was before.

Now, things were different. Except for the getting-out-of-bed thing last night—also a really bad idea—I didn't do stuff like this anymore. It didn't feel right to have adventures when adventures only seemed to cause problems.

I glared at Rafael. Part of me wanted to take back the bracelet and throw it at his face for making me do something that I hadn't wanted to do. The other part of me sorta wanted to thank him for making me do it and give him a super big hug and not let go for a long, long time.

Only that was weird. Obviously not doing adventurous things for a while and then doing two in a row had messed with my brain, big-time. Why would I want to hug Rafael for a super long time? That was something you wanted to do when you liked somebody. And I didn't have a crush on anyone right now, especially not one of my best friends, whose movements reminded me of slimy fish. Even if, up close, he smelled in a strangely interesting way like a garden that hadn't been watered in a while.

Kaya elbowed me in the side. "Look at you," she said. "You're still an Adventurous Girl."

She knew all about the way Mom and I used to be. She was our official photographer that time we climbed to the top of the unbelievably tall outdoor rock wall in Lincoln Park, and that time we took an improv class at Second City, and when we went in a real race car at the Chicagoland Speedway.

"I'm not an Adventurous Girl," I said. Just because I'd gotten a bracelet down from a high place—and done the sneaking-out thing last night that no one needed to know about—it didn't mean anything had changed.

"Oookay," said Kaya.

I gasped. Something was coming out of her head.

No. It wasn't. It couldn't be.

Yes. It was. It definitely was.

"What?" Kaya asked.

"Nothing," I said.

I miss the way she was, said her bubble.

Too bad, I almost said back, even though Kaya hadn't actually said anything. I was different now, and everybody was just going to have to be okay with that.

Then it hit me. The fact that I wanted to talk back to a bubble. The fact that there was another bubble, period. It wasn't just a one-time thing, and it definitely wasn't my imagination.

I breathed in sharply. The bubbles were real.

5

RAINBOW INSIDES

SO IT WAS SETTLED: I WASN'T IMAGINING IT. I COULDN'T be. You couldn't imagine something that crazy twice in a really short amount of time, unless you were living in 1692 in Salem and you had a really active imagination and everyone thought you were a witch because of it. Just like Pratik's, Kaya's bubble had three poofy white dots going from her head to the bigger bubble, and the words inside were small but readable and appeared one by one. And Kaya seemed to have no idea that they were there.

"Hey, Sophie, that was awesome how you got that bracelet," Viv Carlson said as she walked by.

"Uh-huh. Thanks." I couldn't concentrate on anything right now, especially not Viv Carlson, and especially not the bubble over her shiny Viv Carlson head that said: *My project is going to be amazing. Everything I do is amazing! I have the most perfect life!*

What was happening? I felt my forehead, expecting it to be as hot as the Great Chicago Fire of 1871, but it was a totally normal temperature.

"You guys don't happen to see anything up there, do you?" I asked Kaya and Rafael.

"Uh . . . like the ceiling?" asked Rafael. "I do see that. It looks very ceiling-y today."

Kaya laughed. "The ceiling-est," she agreed.

"So you don't see anything else?"

Rafael gave me a strange look. "Do *you* see something else? Also, we really need to hurry. Come on."

So I was the only one who saw the bubbles. Part of me wanted to tell my friends, but we were already going to be late for our classes. And I should tell Mom first, anyway. She'd want to know something major like this before anyone else, and it was the least I could do after everything else I'd done.

The rest of the day went by in a blur. I didn't see any more bubbles, which was kinda weird, but I looked for them everywhere. At least the Shavonna bracelet thing was a good excuse when people asked me why I was looking up so much. *Just looking for more jewelry to save,* I said. Obviously.

When I got home, I was careful to take the elevator and to quietly slip into our place. Most condos in Chicago didn't have an elevator, but our condo did because it was so tall and was pretty new. Mom liked to remind me that we got really lucky—we never had to take the stairs, where we'd probably run into a certain person.

Her idea of luck was way different than mine. If we were actually lucky, I wouldn't have caused Pratik to ditch us in the first place. We'd be able to use the stairs *or* the elevator whenever we wanted and even have races where one of us took one thing and the other person took the other.

When I got inside, Mom was lying on the couch, a giant stack of magazines beside her. Her BFF Britta wrote articles for every magazine in the world, it seemed like, and she was always dropping off extra copies so Mom would have them handy for when her brain needed a break from work. She had started working at home as a website designer person. Well, I was about to give her the ultimate brain break. I hoped. I never really knew how Mom's brain would react anymore.

"So, Mom," I said, in the most casual voice I could, "something weird's been happening since last ni—since yesterday."

"Oh?" She set down whatever she was reading.

My heart thumped a lot all of a sudden, so I looked at

all the different parts of Mom's face instead of her eyes to make the nerves go away. I looked at her long brownish-blondish bangs that went from her head to the tippy tops of her eyebrows. I looked at the shiny silver stud in her nose, her dangly beaded earrings, and the freckles dotted across her cheeks. Then, finally, when I could breathe normally again, I looked at her eyes and started to talk.

"I'm kinda seeing these bubble things. You know, like the thought bubbles in cartoons? Those. Only above actual people's heads."

Mom raised her eyebrows and sat up a little straighter. "You're . . . What?"

"Bubbles," I repeated.

"Bubbles?"

"Yeah."

"Like, above whose heads, exactly?"

That was her first question?

I couldn't say Pratik. After I was done being in trouble for getting out of bed, she'd want to know every little detail about what he looked like and seemed like and blah blah blah. It was so weird, how she could hate somebody's guts but also want to know every little thing about those guts at the same time. We'd be here all night having this talk, and I really didn't want to have it at all. I just wanted things to be better.

Mom gave me a get-on-with-it kind of look, so I got on with it.

"Like Ms. Wolfson," I blurted. "And Kaya and Viv Carlson."

"When did you see Ms. Wolfson?"

Crud.

"In the morning, on my way out."

Lying made me feel bad, but telling the truth would be way worse.

"And were there words in the bubble?"

Crud again.

"Yeah. They just said some stuff about some stuff."

Great, Sophie. Awesome answer.

"Well . . ." Mom scratched her chin and tucked a ringlet of hair behind her ear. "That's pretty weird, Soph. Are you bored? Stressed? Have you been eating anything different?" She glanced over toward the kitchen, like that would tell her the answer.

"No," I said. "I mean, I don't think so."

The only thing different about food was the fact that I *wasn't* eating Pratik's cooking. I sighed. Mom was good at pancakes, but if you wanted anything else, well, you were kinda out of luck.

"I don't know, Soph," Mom said. "I've never heard of anything like this. Maybe we should go to the doctor."

My whole body tensed up. What if something was really wrong with me?

Mom put her arm around me and squeezed, and I took a long breath. "Okay," I said.

"It's going to be fine. I'll call her now to see if she can work you in." Mom gave me a tiny smile. I could tell she didn't really know if it would be fine, but it almost didn't matter. She was *smiling*. And even with all the bad stuff going on, that little fact made my insides feel like a rainbow.

6

FALSE ALARM

THE FIRST DOCTORS ON RECORD WERE THE ANCIENT Egyptians. They believed that evil spirits got inside your body and that's what made you sick. To help you get healthy again, they'd make you eat something that smelled really nasty, hoping the evil spirit would get grossed out and leave.

Medicine has come a long way since then, but I'd almost rather have eaten something that smelled gross than have to sit there any longer.

"The good news," Dr. Peterson said that afternoon, "is that everything looks fine, physically. Now, I could put in an order for a CT scan or a PET scan, but I think the results would probably come back negative, and I don't want you to have to do that unnecessarily."

"Isn't being negative a bad thing?" My voice was much squeakier than normal.

She smiled. "You'd think so, but not in the medical world. That just means that you don't have any of the ailments we would be checking for."

She scribbled something down on a notepad and handed it to Mom.

"This is the number of my friend Dr. Carter. He's a child and adolescent therapist in Logan Square. I think he may be able to provide more appropriate services for this type of situation."

A therapist? I looked at Mom, but it was almost like her eyes were trying to avoid mine. Weren't therapists for people with, like, serious problems? Kaya went to one because of how she was so scared of so many things. I think the therapist helped her, but still. Couldn't I just go to the school guidance counselor? That would be sorta like the same thing, wouldn't it? Just less . . . therapist-ish.

"You think that would help Sophie?" Mom asked.

"I do," said Dr. Peterson.

Didn't anyone want to know if Sophie thought it would help Sophie?

I stood up and stretched a little to help them remember I was still there. It was the worst thing ever when adults acted like you didn't exist, especially when they were talking about you.

"I see a bubble right now, in case anyone's interested," I said. That got their attention pretty quick. And I wasn't making it up. While Dr. Peterson had been talking, the bubble slowly formed over her head. Then the words came, one at a time.

"Oh?" Dr. Peterson looked worried. I'd be worried, too, if there was a bubble over my head that said what hers did. "And what does it say?"

I tried to make eye contact with Mom again. Back when she wasn't so sad all the time, when we were the Adventurous Girls and did everything there was to do and had all the adventures we could, we could also read each other's minds. Well, it was more like she could read mine. She always knew what I was thinking. So if I was shooting her this same look back then, she'd know right away that I was trying to ask whether or not I should tell the truth, because if I did, this could get really awkward really fast. She'd flash me some kind of look back, either her yes-do-it look or her maybe-not-the-best-idea face, and then I'd know and I'd do what she said and it would be the right thing to do because one thing about Mom was that she was always, always right.

Always.

But not anymore, because her face didn't even understand that my face was asking a question. I was on my own.

They both looked at me, waiting. My face felt hot and I wondered if it was possible to choke on your own dry tongue. How could I tell the doctor that her bubble said, *It'll never work*? And how could I tell Mom that I'd basically dragged her here for no reason? She could have been off finding a new job that made her happy or a new boyfriend or something, but instead she was stuck here with me. For nothing.

Some doctor Dr. Peterson was. She didn't know what to do for me and she didn't really truly think what she was suggesting would work, either. I would've been better off with an ancient Egyptian.

At the same time, it was probably hard not really knowing what to do for someone who came to you with a huge problem, especially when the person came to you because you were supposed to be the one who would know what to do.

Maybe I could prove her wrong, show her that it *would* work and that she was actually a pretty good doctor who did have good ideas.

"So you really, *really* think a therapist is the best idea?" I asked. "Like not even the school guidance counselor or something?"

"Guidance counselors are wonderful," Dr. Peterson said, "but they're responsible for so much. Therapists are able to really focus in on you and your individual needs. You can form a substantial relationship that can last well beyond middle school."

She thought I was going to need a therapist well beyond middle school? How messed up did she think I was?

But I wanted to help make her feel better, so instead of asking *Do you think I'm crazy?* like I wanted to, I told her, "By the way, your bubble says *I always give the right advice.*"

Dr. Peterson made a strange face. Mom stared at me like there was a unicorn horn growing out of my forehead.

"Okay then," Mom said. "We'll think about the therapist."

I waited for her to make some kind of Mom face at me that showed she recognized what I had done, making Dr. Peterson feel better like that. Or a Mom face that said, "Don't worry, you're not crazy." Either would have been okay, but neither one showed up.

Mom's reassuring smile from earlier wasn't a fact. It was just a false alarm. I closed my eyes and put my chin in my hands. *Israel became a state in 1948,* I told myself. But even that didn't make me feel better.

7

TRY-ATHLON

THERAPY. WHEN WE GOT HOME MOM SAID IT WAS UP TO me to decide, but the word kept following me around at school the next day like Clark followed Lewis around. (A lot of people think Lewis and Clark were even-steven on their expedition, but Lewis was actually the one in charge.) I tried to push it out of my mind, but it seemed impossible. Finally, when I went over to hang out with Rafael and Kaya at Rafael's apartment after school so we could figure out our risk project, it gave me a break.

Going to Rafael's place always felt like I was showing up in the middle of a party. There was stuff everywhere, and usually fun music was blasting from somewhere in the apartment. Plus, Rafael's kinda reminded me of my dad, which was the coolest thing ever since I'd never even met the guy. I didn't know how you could be reminded of someone you'd never met, but I liked it a lot.

It probably had to do with all the posters covering the walls of his room. Rafael's family was from Argentina, like my dad, and his room was decked out from top to bottom with pictures, postcards, and a giant map so big that it took up an entire wall from the floor to the ceiling. His relatives sent him stuff like that all the time. It was like, *Hey, Rafael, come visit us. Hint, hint.*

I wished someone would send me hints like that, would want me to come visit somewhere cool.

It would be extra great if that someone were my dad, but I wasn't counting on it.

My mom studied in Argentina when she was in college, and she always told people that she got the very best souvenir possible from that trip: me. I think it would have been nice if she also could have gotten some souvenir information about my dad. Like his name, maybe. Or his favorite color, or what he puts on his pancakes—something. But I guess they didn't sell that kind of knowledge at the markets or gift shops.

I eyeballed Rafael's poster of Mount Fitz Roy, this super famous mountain on the border of Argentina and Chile that was first climbed in 1952 by a French and an Italian explorer looking for new adventures. Maybe I would go there someday and my dad would be there, too, and we could go for pancakes (would he like chocolate chip banana, like me, or blueberry, like Mom?) and tell each other everything about ourselves. Maybe he could marry Mom so she wouldn't have to be sad about Pratik anymore. Maybe I could set that up, and then Mom wouldn't even remember that the Pratik thing and the other thing were my fault.

"You okay?" Rafael hurled a cheese ball at my face. It bounced off my nose and landed on his furry red rug. He flung another one my way and I let it fall into my lap. Mom and I used to do goofy things like throwing cheese balls into each other's mouths all the time. I used to be a pro.

"Whatcha thinking about in there?" he asked.

Mom, Dad, Pratik, bubbles, mountains, school, life, pancakes, cheese balls. But I didn't say any of that. Instead, I just shrugged.

Rafael raised his eyebrows. "Hey, remember how you rescued that bracelet at school yesterday? That was a good time."

I giggled. It was so annoying how Rafael always made me giggle when I just wanted to be crabby.

And, okay, fine, maybe it was also a little not-annoying at the same time. Maybe it was kinda interesting. Maybe I kinda wanted to make him giggle, too, like more than usual, even if I couldn't exactly explain why.

"We should reenact it for Kaya," he said.

"Kaya was there!"

"I was definitely there," she agreed.

Rafael groaned. "Work with me, people. Sophie, we are doing it again. Right here, right now. It was awesome and you know it."

I giggled again and he pointed to the top bunk of the bunk beds he shared with his little brother. They didn't go up that high, but Rafael twisted his face into a dramatic OMG! kind of expression, like the top bunk was basically in the sky.

"Oh no! I lost my precious bracelet! What ever will I do?"

I couldn't help it—I full-on grinned, but only for a minute. There was no use fighting Rafael when he was this determined. Plus, it might be weirdly interesting to be that close to him again. My mind drifted to that interesting Rafael-y smell. I didn't know why. I also needed to quit staring at him like any second a bubble was going to pop up that said *I think you smell interesting in a good way, too, Sophie. Let's run away together to a land filled with rainbows and puppy dogs and endless chocolate-chip banana pancakes.*

I tried my hardest to push all that out of my mind. I stood up, took a deep breath, and felt his hands around my waist. My heart got a little thumpy like it had the first time, which was weird because I wasn't going very far off the ground this time.

Rafael lifted me up and I reached for the imaginary bracelet.

"Victory!" Rafael yelled. Kaya laughed and cheered. I sighed and tried to smile. Yeah, this was maybe a little fun, but we should probably be figuring out our risk project instead of doing stuff like this. And I didn't really like doing stuff like this anymore, anyway.

I tried to look at Kaya, but something was in my way. Something white and poofy and bubbly, just hanging out next to me, right above Rafael's head. Another one? Now? Why? I sucked in a big breath and grabbed Rafael's shoulders as hard as I could to keep myself from falling. And then I read it.

Please don't let me mess this up, it said. I bit my lip and stared at it. What didn't he want to mess up? Lifting me? Making me laugh?

"I want to come down," I said. My whole body felt hot, like I was going to melt any second unless someone got me to the ground, fast.

Why did he care so much about not messing anything up, anyway? It was almost like he cared in a different-than-best-friend kind of way.

It was almost like . . . I don't know, like he liked me or something. Like, *liked* me.

Rafael finished lowering me, and I sat down on the floor and took a breath. My skin was this really light brown color, but I still got super red sometimes and people could totally tell. Right now, my face felt like it was even redder than the carpet, and the carpet was brighter than a whole carton of strawberries.

"Next order of business," Rafael said, like there was a checklist of things we needed to do this afternoon and lifting me up was number one. He popped a couple cheese balls in his mouth. Instead of chewing, he moved one to the inside of each cheek. He looked like a chipmunk, which he happened to know I thought was one of the cutest animals on the planet.

Interesting.

"Our risk project," Kaya finished for him. "Our risk project is the next order of business." They gave each other a look and nodded, and then they looked at me. "Rafael and I talked," Kaya said, "and we had an idea."

"Uh, okay?"

My red face had calmed down, but my heartbeat sure hadn't. Why did I get the feeling I wasn't going to like what she was about to say?

Kaya twirled a big chunk of her hair around her fingers. If I was nervous to hear what she was going to say and she was nervous to say it, it definitely couldn't be good.

"Tell me," I said.

But she didn't. She just twirled her hair some more and stared at the floor.

"Uh ay-aff-a-on," Rafael said through his chipmunk cheeks.

I looked at Kaya for translation.

"A triathlon," she whispered.

"No, really," I said. "It's okay, tell me. What's your idea?"

Rafael chewed a little and swallowed the cheese balls. "A triathlon," he repeated. Then he popped five more into his mouth.

I laughed, not sure which was funnier: his super chipmunk-y chipmunk face or the idea.

"That makes no sense. You," I pointed to Rafael, "never learned to ride a bike. And you," I pointed to Kaya, "are scared of a lot of things, especially water and swimming. And me . . ." I stopped. I didn't want to talk about me.

"We know those things aren't easy for us," Kaya said. "That's why it's a risk."

I looked back and forth at both of their faces. Their faces looked back at me.

"You guys are serious about this?"

They nodded, and my whole mouth went dry. I didn't know what to say. A long time ago, I would've loved to do a triathlon. Mom used to do them all the time, and I would always go watch, and sometimes she'd let me run the last part with her. I wasn't actually that good at sporty things—my feet always went all goofy when I tried to run—but the old me wouldn't have cared. She would've tried all the sporty things anyway, and if she fell over and broke a bone or ten, she wouldn't care, because she'd be happy to have had the adventure and the fun.

I wasn't like that anymore, though. I just didn't want to be.

"Or," I said, "we could do something else."

"Like?" Kaya asked.

Crud.

I glanced at the almost-empty bowl of cheese balls. "Want me to go get more snacks?"

They both shook their heads, so I tried changing the subject again. "How about that weather? It's very . . . weather-y today, don't you think?"

"Sophie Elizabeth Mulvaney," Rafael said.

I had no idea how he could go from funny chipmunk guy to serious I'm-gonna-use-your-whole-name guy in two seconds, but he was pretty talented. And pretty cute. And seriously, what was wrong with my brain? He was not cute! He was Rafael!

"Listen." He leaned in a little closer to me, and my

stomach did a weird, bouncy, floppy thing. It was probably just reminding me that it hadn't actually gotten any cheese balls. "We read about this kids' race that's happening in April at Bridgemont Beach. You don't have to go, like, crazy marathon-y distances. There's only a small chance it will kill us."

Kaya elbowed him hard in the guts.

"Sorry. I mean, the chance that it will kill us is not overly large."

Kaya rolled her eyes, but she smiled, too, even though a part of her probably *was* worried that the triathlon would kill her. After all, swimming in a big, deep lake was pretty serious business—especially if you were totally afraid to do it.

"You used to live for stuff like this," Rafael told me. "Remember? You used to love trying new things and having adventures. Like rescuing bracelets. You wouldn't have thought twice about that. And don't get me wrong, we totally like the amazingness that is Sophie the Regular—we like you however you are—but we had a meeting and we decided that we also really miss Sophie the Adventurous Girl."

Kaya nodded along, and I looked from her to Rafael and back. I didn't know whether to be offended they thought I was so regular now or excited that they thought I used to be so cool. Either way, they were right about one thing—I *was* different. And maybe a tiny part of me missed Sophie the Adventurous Girl, too, even though she did a lot of bad things.

"We'd be there with you every step of the way," Kaya said. She twirled her hair around her fingers again, and a bubble popped up over her head.

I can do it, but only with Sophie's help, it said.

I twisted my hands together in my lap and picked off some nail polish that'd been on there for way too long. Because Kaya was afraid of so many things it was a pretty huge deal that she was willing to do this.

And Rafael. He wasn't scared, but he probably didn't want everybody knowing he'd never learned to ride a bike. That could be a pretty embarrassing thing to admit at school. And even when he acted all goofy and pretended nothing embarrassed him, I knew, deep down, that things probably did.

But they both were cool with doing this race because they thought it might make me happy, somehow. They were doing this for *me*. The least I could do for them was agree to do it.

I swallowed hard. "Okay," I said, even though I ran with the speed of a dead snail and the coordination of a spider with eight left feet.

"Okay?" Rafael's face lit up like I'd agreed to do his homework for a month.

"Yeah, okay." I bit my lip. Could we actually pull this off? But their faces were hopeful. They really wanted me to do this. And I really wanted them to be happy.

"Three best friends each doing a race with three parts," I said. "It is kinda perfect for us."

They both grinned.

"It's going to be great," I said, trying to hide my shaky hands and gulpy throat.

And I wasn't even lying that much. It *would* be great. It had to be.

8

ROCKS

THE GOOD NEWS WAS THAT NOW MY MIND HAD SOMETHING else to think about besides the bubbles and the possible therapist.

The bad news was that I'd agreed to do a triathlon, and now I felt like throwing up.

I was worried about a lot of things. Mom's reaction. My eight left feet. All the practicing we'd have to do when none of us really knew what we were doing. But for some reason, my thoughts kept going to Kaya. I was worried about Kaya being worried, even though Kaya's fears were actually what made the three of us friends in the first place.

In second grade, I was best friends with Mom, Kaya was best friends with the teacher, and Rafael was best friends with himself. We barely looked at each other until a field trip to the rock store.

The thing about rock stores is that they're not very exciting unless you're really into rocks. We were learning about them in science, so I guess we were into them, but we kind of had to be into them or else. But the place was boring. It didn't have a rock amusement park or a rock playground or anything to do except look at rocks and not buy them unless you were Viv Carlson and your mom had given you like a zillion dollars and you could walk around in the same glamorous rock necklaces the teachers wore and make everyone else feel like a loser.

So we stood around and looked at rocks. And then this girl who never said anything and always sat twirling her hair and staring at her shoelaces started crying. Like, thick, heavy, the-world-is-ending tears. Right in the middle of the not-so-rockin' rock store. Was she literally bored to tears? Was she sad that she couldn't buy any of the weird rocky souvenirs? What was the deal?

I grabbed her without thinking about it and dragged her to a corner of the store. My teacher gave me a nod and a smile, like I was doing a helpful thing. I liked being helpful almost as much as I liked not having to listen to the Rock Lady talk about rocks.

"What's wrong?" I whispered.

"Please don't make me do anything," she whispered back.

"Huh?"

"You're the girl always hanging upside down on the monkey bars."

I looked around. Were there monkey bars in the store that I hadn't noticed? Because that would be awesome.

"I mean at recess."

"Oh." I had no idea what that had to do with anything.

"I'm scared," she said.

"Of monkey bars?"

"Yup. And of here."

I looked around, trying to find something scary, but all I saw were rocks.

"I don't like field trips. I like to stay at school. I know what's going to happen at school."

"But nothing is going to happen here. Nothing."

She giggled a little.

"Well, maybe that guy is going to hurt himself, but that's really it." I glanced over at the boy spinning around in circles, staring at a fancy clock made out of rocks hanging from the ceiling like it was putting a magical spell on him. That boy looked like fun. Why had I never noticed him before?

"Come on." I offered Kaya my hand. "You can stand by me and everything will be okay."

I guess I shouldn't have made promises I didn't know for sure I could keep, because after I got the teeniest of smiles on her face, that fun boy plowed right into us, and we fell down, and then some fancy rocks next to us fell down, and we all got in Very Big Trouble, and I swore I would never ever talk to That Boy ever again or even go near him.

But then he came up to us the next day and gave Kaya and me our very own rocks that had SORRY written on them with chalk, and after that, we pretty much became best friends.

And now we were all going to try a triathlon.

Kaya the Scared Rock Store Girl would be super proud of herself.

If Kaya the Somewhat Less Scared Sixth Grader was able to do it.

And if that was going to happen, that meant Adventurous Girl Sophie was going to have to show up and help her, but what if I tried to bring her back and it turned out she wasn't there?

I was going to need to totally concentrate on the race, which meant I couldn't be stressed out about anything else.

I took out my phone and wrote a text to Mom as fast

as I could, and then I hit send before I could change my mind. I want to go to the therapist.

You got it, girl. Proud of you ☺, she wrote back.

If we were going to do this triathlon, the bubbles had to go.

9

TEN P.M.

EVEN THOUGH IT HAD BEEN A WHOLE WEEK SINCE I'D seen it, I couldn't get Pratik's bubble out of my mind. He missed us. He really missed us, like how we missed him. So why wasn't he doing anything about it? And why weren't we?

I needed more information. For Mom. And maybe a little for me, too.

That's what I told myself as I snuck out for the second time. It wasn't breaking the rules; it was research.

"Stay in bed," said Mom. "Love you."

I waited until I heard her door close and her imaginary lock lock, then I waited for half an hour before slipping out of bed and pulling on my blue bathrobe. This time I threw a coat on over it, too. Mom would be proud of me for that. Protecting myself from frostbite and everything. I gave myself a pat on the back. Maybe you have to do those kinds of things for yourself, sometimes, like if your mom's asleep, which she was. I made sure there was no light coming from underneath her door.

I went outside and ran to my trusty tree, practically twisting my ankle on my way. I stopped and gave it a quick rub. How did that even happen? Maybe it was my own fault for trying to move too fast. I should have known better. When my feet ran, trouble followed.

I kept going—slowly—and noticed that there was a big FOR SALE sign in front of the condo next door. Maybe Pratik could move there while he and Mom sorted everything out; then he'd be at least a little farther away.

When they broke up, Mom and Pratik got into a big you-move-out-no-*you*-move-out fight. They thought I was busy with Kaya and Rafael, but the truth was that all three of us were in my room, our ears pressed against the door, listening to every word. Also eating cheese balls.

"I've lived on this block for seven years," Pratik said. "I have seniority. I got here first."

"I have a daughter," Mom said. "She goes to school around the corner. I'm not going to uproot her right after the start of sixth grade."

"You uproot her all the time," he said.

"I uprooted her *once*." Mom's voice got louder. "When we moved here from our tiny apartment *two blocks away*. That's not uprooting—that's progress! And you only moved into this building a year before we did, when it opened. That's barely seniority."

They went back and forth for what felt like hours. It might have actually been hours, because I remember when I finally pried my ear away from the door it was numb, like that same kind of feeling your foot gets when it falls asleep. Only it turns out that it's a lot harder to wake up an ear than a foot.

Since they couldn't agree on who would move, no one did. And I don't know much about major life decisions, but I feel like that was maybe not the best one they could have made. I would have rather moved if that meant Mom could act normal again.

Now Pratik's light was on, like I knew it would be. He was on the couch facing the TV, and there was so totally something bubbly coming out of his head. I scooted a little closer, but—holy pancakes!—what was that? I whipped around and tried to figure out where the crunching sound was coming from, but it was impossible to tell. I held my breath and stood as still as I could as the footsteps got louder. Maybe whoever it was wouldn't see me, or they'd think I was another tree or something. A really short tree, but a tree. Maybe a shrub. Whatever.

"Ahhhh!"

I slapped my hands over my mouth and turned around to see who'd tapped me on the shoulder and scared the living pancakes out of me.

"Sophie, calm down! It's me, Ms. Wolfson. What are you doing out here all by yourself in the middle of the night?"

I let out a long, chilly breath.

"It's like ten, Ms. Wolfson. It's late, but it's not the middle of the night."

"When you're old like me, that's exactly what ten p.m. is."

I giggled. "Then what are you doing out here?"

She tucked some of her long silver hair behind her ears. "Sometimes I like going for quick walks before bed to clear my head. It's nice to be in the dark for a bit." Then she held up a flashlight and grinned. "Of course, it's not smart to be *completely* in the dark." She took a step toward the stairs. "I'm heading in. You coming? Your mother must be expecting you."

"Nah. My mother doesn't even know I'm gone. She's in her room."

Locked in her room, I almost added.

"Then who's that?" Ms. Wolfson pointed to a dark figure standing at the top of the steps.

I gulped and slowly turned my head, even though I knew exactly who it was without having to look.

Mom.

10
WEIRD WHIMPERS

MAYBE IT WASN'T MOM. MAYBE I WAS IMAGINING THINGS.
It was close to droopy-eyelid time, and droopy-eyelid time can lead to lots of confusing, wrong things.

But then I heard her voice.

"Sophie. Elizabeth. Mulvaney."

Oh yeah, that was definitely Mom. And she did not sound happy.

She was in her pajamas, robe, and Minnie Mouse slippers, which were the same as mine but a little bigger. (We got the same ones when we went to Disney World, as a souvenir to remember how we chased Minnie into the bathroom because the line to meet her was out of control.) Now Mom's eyes and the skin under them were as red as the bow on Minnie's head. They were puffy, too, like she hadn't slept in a really long time. Of course, Mom's hair was perfect no matter what time it was or how much sleep she got. She was one of those people who could run a hand through it and it would magically fall into place like she was in a commercial for shampoo.

"Get over here right now," she said, and I slowly walked toward the stairs. Ms. Wolfson followed close behind. She was probably scared of Mom, too. Don't be fooled by the flowy hair with all the curls always behaving perfectly—Mom could be really terrifying when she wanted to be.

"Hi, Ms. Wolfson," she muttered as we all made our way into the building.

"Hi, Molly." Ms. Wolfson shot Mom a sideways smile, then turned her flashlight off and went inside. "Hey, Sophie," she whispered to me. "I miss our sleepovers. It's been way too long. Let me know if you ever want to get creamed in cribbage sometime."

"Let me know if *you* want to get creamed," I said. Obviously it had been so long that she'd forgotten who the champion was.

"I'm always here," Ms. Wolfson said to me. But it was weird—as she said it, she looked right at Mom. But then her gaze went back to me. "You girls have a good night."

"You too," I told her.

Mom didn't say anything. She just pulled me into the elevator.

. . .

Mom wasn't a yeller or anything, but I was sorta expecting her to start shouting at me when we got inside. I definitely deserved it. But it was worse—she barely said anything at all. Didn't even look at me. When we got to our door, she unlocked it and went straight in. Then she said, "I know you're seeing bubbles and it's weird and scary and stressful, but that doesn't make it okay to do exactly what I asked you not to. I'm really disappointed," and then she went to her room before I could say anything. She didn't tuck me back in, didn't pull the covers up to my chin and tell me to stay put, didn't lock the imaginary lock and throw away the imaginary key. She just went into her room and that was it. Not knowing exactly what to do, I went to mine, too.

But I couldn't sleep. I could barely even close my eyes for two seconds before they popped open again. Did parents get some kind of book when they had kids that said *Telling your kids you're disappointed will make them feel way worse than if you're just mad*? Because I felt more rotten than the eggs in our fridge that were going bad because no one had turned them into pancakes.

Since sleeping wasn't going to happen, I got up out of bed and went into the living room, to the big, tall white cabinet, and took out Mom's box that she kept on the bottom shelf. The box was filled with old posters, decorations, numbers from races, and a lot of other stuff that used to be hung up in the living room. I don't think Mom ever won any of the races, but she finished them, and that's what the announcer people were always saying was most important. So why did she hate them so much now? And it wasn't just races. She hated *doing stuff*, period. Except for moping around. She was really good at moping around. I was anti-adventures now, but I wasn't anti-everything.

I shoved the box back where it belonged, knowing I should get back to my room before Mom heard me. But I didn't make it to my room, because there was some weird whimper sound coming from hers. I pressed my ear up against Mom's door. It had been a long time since I'd done this. There had been all the conversations and fights with Pratik I'd eavesdropped on, but I'd never eavesdropped on Mom being by herself. Maybe that was a good thing, though. It didn't sound like she was having very much fun.

Was this what she did at night after I went to bed? I

always thought she read more magazines or something—seriously, BFF Britta gave us a never-ending supply—not just sat there making weird, sad-sounding noises. I sat down with my ear pressed up against the door and listened. How could I have done this to her? She was already upset because of everything I'd done, and then I'd gone and made it worse by sneaking out.

I reached for her doorknob, but then I pulled back. I opened my mouth, but then I closed it. Everything I thought of saying or doing seemed stupid, and not being able to come up with anything made me mad at myself. I should be able to do *something*, because Mom always knew what to do for me when I was sad or mad, and now was my chance to really help her, and I couldn't. Think. Of. Anything.

I was an even worse daughter than I had thought.

So instead of opening the door and saying something helpful and brilliant and amazing, the kind of thing that would make her tears disappear like the bubbles did after I read them, I just kept on sitting there, trying and trying and trying to think of something, until my eyes eventually got so heavy that they closed and stayed that way until the morning.

11
UN-MANIFESTING DESTINY

ON SATURDAY I HAD MY FIRST THERAPY SESSION.

"We have a *lot* to do," I said as I unfolded the list I'd made on the bus ride over with Mom. "One, I need to know how to cheer up a sad mom. Two, I need to bring back my adventurous self, but the kind of adventurous self who doesn't mess up and ruin things. Three, I really need to make these bubbles go away."

I tucked the list back into my pocket. Maybe I should've said something more like *hi* when I met my therapist for the first time, but I didn't want to waste time. I needed to know how I could help Mom. Falling asleep outside her door hadn't done anything good for either of us, and neither had my super awkward apology first thing in the morning. She'd been cool about it—she said it was okay; she knew the bubble business must be tough for me, but that didn't mean I could break the rules. Then she gave me a little hug. Still, the whole thing left me with a big headache—but a bigger sense of determination. This mess had to be fixed, and it had to be done today, before anything got worse.

"Oh, and do you think I'm crazy?" I added. "Is there something really wrong with me? My friend goes to a therapist, and she's not crazy, but . . . I don't know." I squirmed around in the fluffy brown chair where he'd told me to sit. It was giant and had all these squishy pillows, and you'd think it would be the comfiest thing on the planet, but it didn't feel much better than the hard floor outside Mom's room.

"It's nice to meet you, too." Dr. Carter laughed. His voice was soft and friendly, kind of like what I imagined a llama would sound like if a llama could talk. If I weren't totally nervous about this, I might think that he reminded me of a llama, and I might think that was sort of awesome.

Dr. Carter was a giant dude who kinda reminded me of Walter Payton, only he was even taller. (I knew all about Walter from when Mom did a TV report on the most famous Chicago Bears players ever in the history of Chicago Bears. He was one of the best running backs of all time.) I had pictured therapists to be little old ladies who knitted and had cats and played bingo and stuff, so it was a major surprise when Dr. Carter turned out to be such a big guy with a llama-like voice.

Maybe that wouldn't be the only surprise today. Maybe he'd be like, "Surprise! The bubbles were actually an early April Fools' joke. In fact, everything that's happened the past few months was an early April Fools' joke. Gotcha!"

But he didn't say that. Instead, Dr. Llama looked down at the clipboard in his lap, and then he looked up at me. "First of all, no, Sophie, you are not crazy. I don't really like that word, anyway. What is crazy? Everyone has problems, tough stuff they have to deal with. Does that mean we're all crazy? You are brave, Sophie. You've entered into a new situation here without knowing much about it other than the fact that it might help you. Not everyone is willing to put in the time and the work."

I gave him a look. Work? No one had said anything about work. Wasn't he the one with the job here? He was supposed to listen to me and fix everything.

Dr. Llama leaned forward. "We can discuss whatever you want, but first I have a few questions I need to ask you, okay? First, how are you?"

"Uh, fine?" That was a pretty normal question in life, but here it felt like a weird one to start with, especially after everything I'd just said. He didn't respond, so I asked it back to him, since that was the polite thing. "How are you?"

He blinked, smiled, and wrote something down.

"Have you ever tried to hurt yourself?"

Well, that was a weird answer to the question. Most people just said "fine" or "good."

"No, of course not," I said. "I hurt myself all the time, but I've never *tried* to. It just happens whenever I run. Like this one time—" I paused. "Wait, why are you asking me that?"

"This is just protocol," he said. "Kind of like a set of rules I have to follow. I have to ask new clients the same questions. Just go with it, okay?"

I nodded and crossed my legs. The chair still wasn't comfy.

Dr. Llama continued. "Do you ever hear voices?"

No, but I see words, I wanted to say. *Can we talk about that now, since, y'know, it's why I'm here?*

After about a million more weird questions, he got to a topic that actually made sense. "So, tell me about your family."

I sat up a little straighter. "My family? Well, there's me and Mom, and that's pretty much it."

I thought of Mom in the waiting room. I hoped she wasn't too bored.

Dr. Llama looked at me like he was waiting for more.

"There used to be Pratik, but I accidentally made him and Mom break up. Kinda like I made Mom lose her job."

Yeesh. Saying it all out loud like that made it seem a gazillion times worse than it already was. I was like the United States after they'd come up with Manifest Destiny (the idea that everybody else's land should actually be theirs) and started snatching up all the places they could get. Only instead of stealing stuff, I just messed things up. I had to find a way to un-manifest destiny before it was too late.

"How did you make your mom lose her relationship and her job, exactly?"

Dr. Llama's brown eyes met mine, but they weren't judgy. I had never really talked about this with anybody before, maybe because I was scared of seeing mean eyes from other people like the ones I gave myself whenever I looked in the mirror.

"I told Mom something Pratik told me not to tell her and they got in a fight and broke up. And the job thing . . . ugh." I squeezed my eyes shut. I really, really didn't want to see the memory in my brain, but there it was, as clear as the words in everybody's bubbles.

Everything happened in slow motion that day, like in one of those scary movies where you know exactly what's coming but there's nothing you can do to stop it.

I was in the bathroom, painting a blue streak in my hair. I'd wanted one forever, and Mom finally said it was okay. It didn't get much more adventurous than blue hair. So I was doing that, only it turns out it's a lot harder to dye your own hair than people online make it look. For one thing, it was sorta impossible to reach certain places on my own head. For another thing, it felt like my head was on fire.

I grabbed the bowl of hair dye and sprinted (badly) out into the living room. I yelled for Mom to come help, but she didn't answer. My head was so hot! This was so not working! I spun around to face the other direction, but I still didn't find Mom.

I did find her phone, though.

Which I only knew because of the loud thudding sound it made when I knocked it off the table.

It's a pretty bad thing to break your mom's phone. It's an extra bad thing to break your mom's phone and then find out later, once she's gotten a new one and your head is back to a normal temperature, that she missed a Super Important Call from work, the kind of call she needed to answer right away because it was about covering a big news story that was happening right that minute.

It was the kind of call Mom could get in Big Trouble for not answering.

And then she did. She went in for a really, really long talk with her boss.

And when Mom came home from that really, really long talk, she didn't have a job anymore.

Because of stupid feet, and stupid adventures, and me.

I took a big breath after I was done telling the story to Dr. Llama. There was something so, so awful about saying it out loud. But there was also something kind of okay about saying it out loud, too.

If I could pull off this triathlon business, maybe it would show Mom that I could control my feet, that she didn't have to worry that I'd do something like that ever again. And I'd show her I could be adventurous without being dumb, too. Maybe there were actually lots of good things that could come out of the triathlon, if I could get myself to do it.

Dr. Llama wrote some stuff down. Then he said, "Thank you for sharing that with me, Sophie. Now, would you like to tell me about the bubbles?"

Finally!

I closed my eyes and tried to picture one. "They're kinda like a little white cloud with words inside. And three little circles that lead from the cloud to the person's head. And the person has no idea that it's there."

That was the weirdest part, how the bubble was literally right above someone's head and the person didn't have a clue. It'd be like not knowing that you were wearing sunglasses or that you were standing on the ground. What if there was a bubble over my head right now?

"You're thinking something." Dr. Llama said this like a statement, but looked like he wanted an answer.

"Just how it's weird that people can't see their own bubble. And their bubble doesn't always make sense. And I'm the only one who can see them."

"That may or may not be the case," he said, sitting back.

"What do you mean? Other people can see them, too? Who? Can you?"

"I mean, sometimes you don't need to see something to be able to see it. I think I may know a thing or two about your bubbles."

"Like what?"

He smiled. "You have to figure that out yourself."

"I have to figure out what you know about my bubbles?"

"No, what you know."

"But I don't know."

"You know. You just don't know that you know."

I made a face. I knew I was confused as heck, but

that was about it. And I didn't know anything about the bubbles—that's why I was here. Duh!

Therapy was supposed to solve my problems, but it was making everything more jumbled up. Maybe Dr. Peterson was right that it would never work.

"Is therapy always this confusing?" I asked.

"Yeah, usually." Dr. Llama laughed. "Think you'll come back?"

I really wanted to make an annoyed face—after all, it had almost been an hour and we'd accomplished nothing—but a giggle escaped instead. And then a tiny smile did, too. What was up with that? He hadn't helped! He admitted this was confusing—and worse, that it was going to be *work*!

So it was really, really weird that I nodded yes.

I felt a little lighter, though. It was like I was in charge of holding a bunch of cool history books that were super heavy, and I was finally allowed to set one down.

Therapy was weird. It was definitely weird.

But maybe it was good, too.

12
SECRETS

IN 1776, A BUNCH OF GUYS (FIFTY-SIX OF THEM, TO BE exact) signed the Declaration of Independence, and they were super excited. They were going to be independent! Woo-hoo! The thing a lot of people don't know is that after all this awesomeness, most of the guys actually went on to have kinda cruddy lives. Some of them lost their homes, and some of them were captured by the British (who were pretty mad at them, to say the least). Their problems were far from over.

Maybe that was how things were doomed to be for me. I'd left therapy feeling kinda floaty and relieved and good, even though I didn't really get why. Mom asked me how it went and didn't say anything else after I told her it was okay, so I spent the rest of the bus ride home wondering if that was how Kaya felt when she left therapy, too. We had never really talked about it in detail before. All I really knew about Kaya's therapist was the fact that she had one.

So the bus ride was okay. But then there was night. And there were more weird whimper noises coming from Mom's room. And I wondered if maybe I should get out of bed again and knock on Pratik's door and tell him about the whimpers if he answered. But then I wondered if telling him would make things worse, and then I remembered how everything I did (or even thought of doing) made things worse.

Eventually, I fell asleep. I have no idea how that happened.

• • •

On Monday when I got to school, I saw more bubbles than I'd ever seen before. It was terrible that so many people were thinking sad, stressed-out things: *I can't. I'll never be able to. There's no way.*

As I walked down the hall to social studies, my head was pounding, like it was filled with secrets and sadness and didn't know what to do with them and couldn't hold them all in. Was everyone secretly upset about something? Wasn't anyone secretly *happy*? Were there really this many things that could—and did—go wrong in the world, even though everybody bopped around all the time like everything was fine? At least Mom was honest about how cruddy she felt. Everybody else was just faking it.

I sat in my seat and buried my head so deep in my hands that I barely even noticed Kaya sliding into the seat next to me.

"Hey, how are you?" she asked.

"Fine," I sighed. "How are you?"

"Good."

I forced myself to sit up. I had slept okay, I guess, but I felt totally wiped out. Was twelve too young to take up coffee drinking? The big Starbucks cup on Mr. Alvarado's desk was calling my name.

"You've been acting weird lately." Kaya undid her topknot and her hair spilled out everywhere. She grabbed a big chunk and spun it around her fingers.

"I know, you and Rafael told me," I said.

Rafael. I broke into a little smile just thinking his name. The cheese-ball chipmunk thing last week had been so funny. Had he always been that funny?

"No, not that. Like you seem sleepy all the time."

I looked into her dark brown eyes and considered telling her. She twirled the hair around her fingers faster and faster. Obviously my acting weird was making Kaya nervous, and she was nervous enough as it was. I couldn't do anything about all the other sad, stressed people, but I could help her.

"Okay." I leaned over so far that I was practically sitting in her seat with her. "Promise not to think I'm insane if I tell you something? It's top secret."

"I won't think you're insane. And of course I won't tell." She let go of a few pieces of hair.

"I've been seeing these weird thought-bubble things over people's heads. They say what the people are really thinking. And people think weird things. And sad things. And it's getting worse. And even my new . . ." I lowered my voice, "therapist didn't know what it was or what I should do."

Kaya let go of her hair entirely, then picked a piece back up, then dropped it again. She grabbed on to her long sweater and wrapped it around her tighter. Then she bent down and pushed her leggings into her boots. This just meant Kaya was thinking. Hair meant nerves. Fiddling meant thinking. What was she thinking about? Was she deciding if she still wanted to be my best friend?

I'm not so sure about this bubble stuff, her bubble answered me. *But I'm too worried about swimming to think about it too much.*

She grabbed her hair again. Poor Kaya. My headache

pounded a little harder as Mr. Alvarado strummed a few notes on his guitar, which meant it was time to be quiet and get started. I looked at Kaya, but she stared straight ahead.

"Buenos días," Mr. Alvarado said. "We're going to dive into chapter thirteen today—the American Revolution continues! But before we do that, let's touch base about our risk projects. What have you been thinking about? What are your ideas? Who wants to share?"

Mohammed raised his hand. "I'm going to go on a roller coaster. I've never been on one before."

Mr. Alvarado nodded excitedly. Viv shot him a way-too-enthusiastic thumbs-up sign from across the room. *I've been on lots of roller coasters. I'm so brave,* her bubble said.

"I'm going to try out for the baseball team," said Cordell. "I've always wanted to be on a baseball team, but I've been scared to try."

People murmured "cool" and "nice" and other things like that. Soon everyone's hands were up.

"Rahama and I are going to join the protests at the animal shelter downtown," said Nora. "They want to turn it into a parking lot!"

"I'm going to give a presentation in a loud voice to the whole class," LaMya whispered.

"Mine's going to be so extremely risky that I can't even say it out loud," said Viv. "It has to do with people," she added, and then she looked right at Kaya and me.

I raised my eyebrows. Did Kaya and I both have something stuck in our teeth? Or did her project . . . have to do with us?

"Miguel and I are going to start a business," said Harrison. "Buy our stuff!" Everybody laughed.

Miguel asked, "It's cool if they don't, though, right, Mr. A.? This project is about taking a risk. It doesn't matter if it works out or not."

"Actually, it matters a lot," said Mr. Alvarado. "This is an assignment. Part of your grade is deciding on your risk and writing an essay about your process. The other part is taking the risk and accomplishing your goal."

The room was silent for a second. He couldn't expect everyone to actually be successful at what they said they would try. It had to be a joke. No offense to Cordell, but I'd seen him throw a baseball in gym class. He wasn't good. And LaMya only ever spoke in a whisper, when she even spoke at all. She'd never be able to speak loudly in front of the whole class. Plus, if Mr. Alvarado could be understanding of all the historical people who didn't achieve their goals, why couldn't he be understanding of his own students?

I thought Kaya would be frantically messing with

her hair after hearing this, but she wasn't. She wasn't messing with her clothes, either. She shot me a sideways smile and slowly raised her hand.

"Sophie, Rafael, and I are all going to do a mini-triathlon," she said. "It's for kids. You bike one mile, run a half mile, and swim . . ."—she gulped—"fifty yards."

"Magnífico!" Mr. Alvarado said. "That sounds like an excellent risk. Are you sure you're up for the challenge?"

Kaya's face turned green and she reached for her hair. *Not at all,* said her bubble. *But I'm sure that I'm going to throw up if I talk about it anymore today.*

"I looked up some of the best training techniques for beginners," I chimed in, trying to take everybody's attention off Kaya. She was only doing this race because of me. It was pretty much my fault her face was this really scary-looking color. "I have a plan to get us ready."

"You do?" Kaya's whole face relaxed. She liked plans. Even ones that didn't totally exist. But she didn't need to know that right now.

"I do," I answered. She smiled with all her teeth and all her braces, and her face went back to its normal dark brown color.

"Well, good," she said with a giggle. "We're gonna need all the techniques we can get."

My head felt a little less poundy than it had when class started. There were a lot of sad and bad things in people's brains near and far, but Kaya knew my secret and she was still here, wanting to do the triathlon with me. Plus, I'd used her bubble to actually help her out a little bit, even though it was my fault she had to have that bubble in the first place. But still. I helped, sorta. And that made me feel more awake than the biggest cup of coffee ever could.

Well, I didn't know that for sure.

But I'd take the risk.

13

FOR THE GLOVES

EVEN THOUGH I WAS FEELING A LITTLE BETTER, VIV'S words bugged me long after class ended. *Mine's going to be so extremely risky that I can't even say it out loud.* Well, how fancy for her. The words from her bubble bugged me, too. *I've been on lots of roller coasters. I'm so brave.* And the mysterious *It has to do with people*, and the way she was looking at Kaya and me like we were exactly the people it had to do with.

Sometimes I wished I liked Viv more. The truth was that she'd never really done anything mean to me. Sure, she was a little braggy about how many activities she did and how many friends she had, and it was annoying how her accessories and hair and face changed like eighty-nine times a day and she knew more people in our school than I knew in the whole world.

But she hadn't done anything bad.

Unless you counted fourth grade.

We were better friends, then. Not best friends or anything, but actual friends who talked to each other and hung out at recess and did all the things that actual friends did. That year, it was a huge deal to cover your friends' lockers with ribbons and bows on their birthdays. And I'd always see Viv at school really early in the morning doing it for everybody. She was like, Super Decorator Girl, leaving no locker un-beautified.

The weird thing was that on Viv's birthday, there wasn't a single thing on her locker. I had assumed that there were a million people who were going to decorate it, so I stayed out of the way. But when I walked by on the way to class, it just looked like a regular old locker.

I didn't really carry spare bows around or anything (and I couldn't ask the one person who did), so I had to think fast. I ripped out a piece of notebook paper, wrote HAPPY BIRTHDAY in bubble letters, and drew the nicest stars and hearts and swirly designs I could in ten seconds.

Later that day at lunch, when she finally saw it, she assumed it was from everybody in her after-school dance class.

Worse, they didn't deny it, even though you'd think they'd be embarrassed to admit that the most a whole group could do was make one boring little sign that wasn't even colored in.

When I told her that it was me, not, like, an entire team's worth of people, she didn't believe me. She acted like she didn't even hear me. Like I wasn't even there.

So maybe she had done something mean to me after all.

Maybe it would have been better if we totally stopped being friends after that, but we still hung out for a while, just not as much. But now everything felt too fakey-fake. Her smiles, her compliments, everything. If I ever saw another bubble over her head, I bet it would say what I already knew: *I want all the attention.*

Well, after I figured out what her project was, she wasn't getting any more from me.

· · ·

After social studies class, Kaya and I walked toward our hallway meeting spot without talking. I didn't know what to say. *Thanks for sticking with me even though I have this weird bubble problem* sounded dorky. *Tell me about your therapist* sounded pushy. I was about to say something about the weather when Viv popped up out of nowhere and rushed right toward us.

"Hey, Kaya!" Viv said. "Your triathlon idea sounds

awesome. I'm really into exercise, too. My mom is a group fitness instructor." *And one day, I could be, too,* said her bubble. *With how talented I am at everything, I can be anything I want.*

"Thanks! That's cool," Kaya said.

I groaned to myself. It was like Viv wanted a medal for being into exercise, and a second one for having a mom who was into exercise. And a third one just for existing.

"Hey, Viv," I said, but what I meant was *I'm standing here too, ya know. How about you tell me about your secret project that has something to do with me? Also, can you stop freaking my BFF out about the triathlon, please? We are already freaked out enough, thank you very much.*

She flicked her eyes to me for half a second, pushed her glasses up on her nose, and then turned back to Kaya.

"Well, I have science, so see you later." And then she waved again and was off.

At least now I didn't have to struggle to figure out what to say to Kaya.

"That was weird," I said as we kept walking.

"I don't know," Kaya said. "I thought it was nice."

"Uh, were we just talking to the same Viv Carlson?"

Kaya laughed. "She's not that bad."

I was about to say something about all the people

throughout history who didn't seem that bad who then ended up doing some seriously bad things, but when we turned the corner and saw Rafael waiting at our meeting spot, I completely forgot what I was going to say.

I burst into a big grin. His face was just regular—it wasn't chipmunk-y or anything—but something about it still made me feel all warm and giggly.

"I have something for you," he told me.

"You do?"

I bit my lip and tried my very hardest not to giggle.

He pulled something out from behind his back. "Ta-da!"

I frowned. The something was paper.

He handed one piece to me and another one to Kaya.

"I printed out our permission slips for the triathlon in the computer lab this morning," he said. "We have to turn them in to ZOOM Athletics by April first, so that gives us almost a month to fill them out. Sophie, since you live the closest, can you drop them off?"

I nodded and glanced at the paper.

ZOOM presents
Chicago Kids Mini-Tri
April 7th, Ages 11–14, 8 A.M.

Adult Tri, 7 A.M.
Bridgemont Beach
The top three finishers in each age group
(kids and adults) will receive a $500 gift
card to ZOOM Athletics and be
featured on Channel 23 at 10 A.M.

"Why yes," Rafael said as he watched us read. "Your eyes are not deceiving you. A five-hundred-dollar ZOOM gift card could be yours! And yours! And mine!"

But I couldn't think about that. "Channel 23," I whispered. This was my chance! Channel 23 used to be Mom's channel. I could finally make up for what I'd done. I probably couldn't make Pratik go out with Mom again, but I could totally get her back in front of the camera.

Maybe if I got to be on TV, even if it was just for a few minutes, she could come on TV with me. After all, important things usually require a parent. Mom had to sign a paper when I got my ears pierced. She had to say okay when I went to a friend's house after school, and she usually took the El train or the city bus with me if I was going somewhere outside of Wicker Park. So if I got on TV, the TV people would probably want her there, too.

And maybe if she got on TV, the TV people would

remember how good she was and they'd give her her job back.

Kaya jabbed me in the ribs. "You okay?" she asked. "Are you seeing . . . one of those things?"

"What things?" Rafael asked.

I gave Kaya a look and she wrapped some hair around her fingers. It wasn't that I didn't want to tell Rafael about the bubbles . . . I just . . . well. Hmm. Maybe I didn't want to tell Rafael about the bubbles. What if he thought I was nuts?

"Hey, tell us why you're so excited about the ZOOM gift card," Kaya said to him. "Please?"

"Nice try. I'm not some little kid where you can just go and change the subject and I'll start talking about something else and forget that you guys are being secretive about something." He kicked the floor with the toe of his sneaker. "Although . . ." his face broke out into a grin. "Okay, fine, since you asked nicely. ZOOM Athletics has those awesome ShiverStoppers wool gloves. All different colors and patterns. They're so warm and soft, it's actually unbelievable."

"Why don't you just go buy some?" Kaya asked.

"Are you kidding? Those things run like a hundred bucks per glove. My parents would never let me spend that kind of money on gloves, even if it's basically for the safety of my hands. Seriously, they're like sticking your hands into their own warm mini-clouds of joy."

Kaya and I exchanged a look, and I could finally let my giggle out without it being weird.

Rafael's face turned serious.

"I don't think we should just train for this race," he said. He put his hands out and looked off into the distance all dramatically, like he was George Washington posing for his official White House portrait in 1797. "I think," he said slowly, "that we should try to win it."

We all looked at each other as we headed toward our classes. Yesterday, I would've laughed at the idea of trying to win. And not just a little giggle laugh. More like a hold-your-sides-fall-on-the-floor-maybe-start-snorting kind of laugh. But now that Channel 23 was involved, and I could really make things right . . . maybe it wouldn't be such a bad thing to try.

"That's impossible," Kaya said. "But I'd probably never be scared of swimming again if I knew I could do it faster than everybody else."

"We should totally try to win it, then," I heard myself say. "For that, and for the chance to be on TV."

And for Mom, I said in my head.

"And for the gloves," said Rafael. The hallway was emptying out. We raced to our classrooms, and as Kaya and Rafael entered theirs, I heard him yell, *"For the gloves!"*

Holy chocolate pancakes. Not only was I doing a triathlon, but I was actually going to try to win one, too.

What was I getting myself into?

14
SPINNING

"WHO ARE WE?" I ASKED WHEN I MET KAYA AND RAFAEL at the front desk of the Wicker Park Athletic (WPA) Club later that afternoon.

"The bike riders!" Kaya and Rafael shouted, like I'd made them practice a thousand times before I even let them into the gym.

"What are we going to do?"

"Bike!" Kaya yelled at the same time as Rafael shouted, "Not die!"

I giggled, but it felt like a fake, Viv Carlson-ish type of laugh. I was trying my very hardest to stay focused on my friends and not on what had happened before I got to the gym, but that was pretty hard. I'd told Mom where I was going and what we were training for, and she'd just stared at me the same way she stared at everything else—like she was looking, but she didn't really see.

"Have fun," she had said in a robot-zombie kind of voice. Then she turned back to *Microbiology Monthly*, a magazine that no way was more interesting than her own daughter and her triathloning.

But it was fine. She just didn't get what a huge deal this was turning into.

The day of the race, though, that was when it would hit her. I could totally picture it: she'd be having a normal, mopey day, and I'd be like, "Mom, come with me," and before she realized what was happening, I'd be doing a whole triathlon, winning it, and getting us both on TV. Before she knew it, she'd find herself saying, "Wow! That was amazing. You've totally reminded me, Sophie, that I used to love races. And having fun." And then her boss would appear and say, "Speaking of having fun, how about starting by taking your old job back?" And then Mom would wrap me in a big hug and say, "I'm so happy," and look at me like she used to. And then Pratik would appear and wrap both of us in a hug and then we'd all go out for pancakes and live happily ever after.

"Hi. Um, Sophie?" Rafael snapped his fingers across my face, and I blinked a bunch of times. Okay, I was getting way too far ahead of myself. Before that whole thing could happen, we had to win the race. Which meant I had to teach Rafael how to bike and we all needed to know how to bike really, really well. Which meant I seriously had to pay attention.

"Sorry," I said. "Just thinking. Anyway, come with me, guys. We're going to a super cool place." I stood on my tiptoes and glanced at the room I wanted to take them into. No one was going in or out, so it was probably still empty like it had been when I checked before my friends got here.

They finished signing and followed me through the lobby. It was so awesome that all our parents belonged to WPA, and now that we were twelve we could use their memberships and come by ourselves.

I grabbed the door handle and sucked in my breath. My official practice plan wasn't quite as detailed as I'd made it seem to Kaya when I'd spoken up in class. Right now, the name of the plan was "Cross My Fingers and Hope This Works Out."

The sign next to the door of the room read SPIN STUDIO. I'd found it when I'd been roaming around, looking for bikes we could use that would be good for beginners like Rafael. At first I thought "Spin Studio" was a fancy way to say "The Twirl-in-Circles Room" (which was something I knew he'd love—even though we didn't hang out in rock shops anymore, the guy still liked to twirl), but when I looked inside, I discovered that spinning actually had everything to do with biking. There were hundreds of bikes—or at least, like, thirty—lined up in rows across the room. The place reminded me of a dance club right out of movies I'd seen on TV. I half expected a disco ball to come down from the ceiling and a pop song to start blasting from invisible floor-to-ceiling speakers at any second.

"This. Is. Awesome," Rafael said as he looked right at me. There wasn't any exercise happening yet, but my hands felt sweaty and my heart was beating fast. He seemed to have forgotten that we were here to ride bikes, because he definitely didn't think biking was awesome.

A bubble formed over his head. *She is awesome.*

I stopped breathing for a second. Maybe he wasn't thinking about the bikes at all. She who? She me? Must be. He thought I was awesome?

He thought. I. Was. Awesome!

And that felt, well . . . awesome.

Why could I suddenly not think of any other words? Why had my brain turned to mush? Why could I not stop asking myself questions in my head in a really excited kind of voice?

Maybe it was time to officially admit that I thought he was awesome, too.

And if I thought he was awesome and he thought I was awesome, what did that mean? With Demarius,

I'd been like, *I like you,* and he'd been all, *Okay, later.* And then we'd hung up the phones and lived awkwardly ever after.

But this was different. This time, the guy might like me back. And what happened then?

I guessed we could figure it out later. For now, we could ride fake bikes.

"There's no class in here for another half hour," I said, pointing to the schedule next to the giant mirror on the wall. "So I thought we could borrow these bikes till then."

Rafael studied them. "Are these things glued to the ground?" He grabbed one and acted like he was pulling on it as hard as he could, and Kaya laughed.

"Don't!" I told him. "I think they probably have a you-break-it-you-buy-it policy around here. Anyway, aren't these great? We can work our way up to the real thing. This will be nice and easy."

Kaya looked at the bike like it was a math problem she was trying to figure out.

"The bikes are different heights," she said. "We should probably find the shortest ones. Unless anyone knows how to adjust them."

We all looked at each other and shook our heads.

"Right. So maybe these?" Kaya pointed to a few that seemed lower to the ground than the others. She tightened her helmet around her neck, and Rafael and I put ours on, too. Wearing a helmet for this felt a little dorky, but I knew the extra safety would make Kaya feel better, even if she already knew how to ride a bike.

We each took a seat on a bike, and it was hard not to jump right back off. I'd forgotten how uncomfortable these things were. There had been so many great inventions throughout history, but no one had created a bike seat that felt like a pillow.

"Well, this has been a fun-tastic time, my friends, but I have to get going. I just remembered, I have a previous commitment with something not painful." Rafael leaped off his bike like the seat was made of hot lava.

"Not so fast, mister." Kaya put a hand on his shoulder and practically pushed him back on. "It takes a minute to get used to it. Just hang on a little longer. Before you know it, you won't even notice."

"I seriously doubt that," Rafael said, but he sat back down. Then he looked at me and rolled his eyes in a joking way, like, *Do you believe this girl?* I smiled and rolled mine back. *I know, right?*

He kept on looking at me, and then Kaya looked, too, and it was almost like they were waiting for something. Which was maybe because they were.

"Oookay," I said, doing my best to pretend that there was more to my training plan than coming into the room, getting on the bikes, and trying to find the secret disco ball that had to be around here somewhere. "So. These are bikes. They have seats, and pedals, and lots of other bikey things. Pretty sweet, right? Did you know that they were invented in 1816? Because they were."

My mind went totally blank. How did you teach someone to ride a bike, anyway? Especially someone who thought you were awesome and made your heart poundy and your mouth giggly and had a serious look of concentration on his face that was also weirdly kinda cute?

"Maybe Rafael should put his feet on the pedals," Kaya offered.

I snapped my fingers. "Yeah! I was just going to say that." I stretched my legs out to where the pedals were. They were kinda hard to reach.

"I'm doing it! I'm riding a bike!" Rafael yelled. He was already pedaling faster than I thought was even possible on these things. If this was the race, he'd be talking on TV by now, and I'd be back by the starting line . . . alone.

"Way to go!" I finally got my feet on the pedals, but every time I moved them, it was like pedaling in quicksand. They felt really twisty, too, like they were going to get tangled up and crash any second. Which was silly, since I was barely even moving. I thought this would be easier than riding a real bike, but it turned out that it was harder—at least harder for me.

A big lump formed deep in my throat. If anyone came in the room, it would look like Rafael and Kaya were teaching *me* to ride a bike—and that they weren't doing that great of a job.

"We should try to stand up," Rafael said, after a few more minutes of him and Kaya being amazing and me being, well, not.

I rolled my eyes and took my feet off the pedals. "Yeah, okay. Then let's do headstands on the handlebars."

Rafael looked like he was considering it. "No, I'm serious. We're basically masters of biking now. And anyway, the bikes are stuck to the ground, remember?"

I did remember. But I also remembered that sitting on the bike—and trying to make the pedals move— was hard enough.

Kaya smiled and stood up like it was nothing. "This is fun," she said. Rafael stood, too. "I'm on top of the world," he shouted. They high-fived each other and looked at me, like they were waiting for something again and I was taking way too long to give it to them.

This time I knew exactly what they were waiting for, but that didn't mean I knew how to do it.

But if they could do it, I could, too, couldn't I? An Adventurous Girl would. And if I was serious about winning the race, I had to give my old self a real chance to make a comeback. And it didn't get much more real than standing up on a bike that you probably shouldn't stand on.

I took a deep breath and stretched my legs until my knees were slightly bent. Slowly and carefully, I arched myself up and over until I was almost as high up as Rafael and Kaya were . . . just in time for them both to plop back down on their seats.

"Really? I just got here." I leaned forward and grabbed the handlebars to steady myself.

Kaya giggled. "I'll come back!" She stood up again and waved to me. Then she sat back down. And got back up. And went down. And got up.

Rafael started doing the same thing.

"Race you guys," he said as he bounced up and down like a kangaroo. "First one to nowhere wins!"

"Come on, Sophie," Kaya said. "Go faster with us!"

I sighed and dared myself to stand up again.

They both went up and down and up and down, faster and faster and faster. They looked like human rocket ships, about to take off and go flying to the moon. I forced myself up, then down, then up. My breath was heavy and my heart thumped a zillion miles a minute, but I kept going even though each movement felt like lifting an elephant. Up. Down. Pedal. Bike. Up. Feet.

Hands. Down. It was hard on my body, but tough for my brain, too. There was so much to remember.

"You got it," Kaya said, so I tried to go even faster still. Up! Down! Up! Down! Down. Down.

Down . . .

And then, somehow, I didn't exactly know how, I was on the ground.

"Ow."

Kaya and Rafael slowed to a stop.

"Um. Did you just fall off a bike that wasn't moving?" Rafael asked.

"But *we* were moving," I said. They got off their bikes and stood next to me. They were both sweaty, but it didn't even look like real sweat. They were glistening. My sweat was smelly and theirs was sparkly and nothing was fair about anything.

"I'm so glad we had helmets on," said Kaya. "You could've gotten really hurt."

I groaned. I *was* really hurt. Maybe not on my head, but just about everywhere else. I sprawled out on the ground next to my terrifying stationary bike of doom, then rolled over so I was on my stomach and closed my eyes.

The room went totally quiet. Maybe everybody had left. Maybe they were too embarrassed to be in the same room with me. I lifted my head and opened my eyes.

Nope, Rafael and Kaya were definitely still there, and they had funny looks on their faces, like they'd been caught doing something bad. Behind them, staring, was a huge crowd of people.

Including the one and only Viv Carlson.

. . .

"Are you okay?" she asked in her fake-nice Viv Carlson voice.

Right. Like she cared.

"I've been teaching spinning for twenty years and I've never heard of anyone falling off one of these. I wonder what she was doing wrong," some lady said. She had to be Viv's mom, the "group fitness instructor," whatever that meant. She had the same orangey-brown hair and annoying singsongy voice as her daughter. Her skin was unbelievably tan, like she'd just dipped her body in a giant carton of orange juice.

I didn't say anything back. I just lay there until I heard another familiar voice. And this one actually sounded nice. "Do you need some help getting up?"

Who was that? I lifted my head as high as it would go.

"Ms. Wolfson?"

"Sophie?"

I made a weird gurgly noise that didn't really mean yes or no. It kinda just meant *Get me out of here, please,* and a second later, her hand was firmly gripping mine.

I knew that I had to get up. That's what people did in this kind of situation. I had to get back on the horse. Or the stationary bike. Or just leave. Or whatever. The point was, I had to get up, because that's what Adventurous Girls did, that's what cool historical people did, and that's what regular people did, too.

Only . . .

A weird thought crossed my mind. Who said that we always had to get up? Why couldn't we lie there if that's what we felt like doing? Now that I thought about it, usually the guys who lay there during battles throughout history were the ones who survived. Mom had been acting like she was lying on the ground for the past five months now, and she was getting by.

But maybe getting by wasn't enough. Wasn't the whole point of this risk project (besides doing it for Kaya and Rafael) to inspire Mom, to remind her how fun it was to have adventures and try new things and *not* spend all day lying around?

This project sure didn't feel very fun right now. Even so, I squeezed Ms. Wolfson's hand and let her pull me up.

"So what were you guys doing here?" Viv asked.

I could feel Ms. Wolfson watching me, even if she was quiet.

"We started training for our triathlon," Kaya said.

"Oh, the one you were talking about in class? The one in April? I'm totally doing that triathlon, too! Look, I have my sign-up sheet right here." She waved it around and around, so much that I felt a little dizzy.

"You're doing it for your risk project?"

"No." She giggled. "Just for fun. I'm doing something more challenging for my risk project."

"And that would be?" I asked, but nobody seemed to hear.

"You should give your sign-up sheet to Sophie," Kaya said. "She offered to go to ZOOM and turn all of ours in."

Viv practically shoved the form into my right hand. My left, I realized, was still clutching Ms. Wolfson's. "Thanks, Sophie! Anyways, I take it you guys don't want to stay for the spin class?"

"Hey now." Rafael stepped forward. He had taken off his helmet and held it above his head like a trophy. "We'll stay for the class if we want to stay for the class. We fear no spinning. We leave no spinning bike unspun. We spin the spinning bikes to spinfinity and beyond." *I am the master of the spinning*, his bubble said. *And*

soon I will be the master of the gloves, and the universe!
Bwahaha.

"Are you serious about wanting to stay?" Kaya asked him. "Because I would do it if you would."

Kaya, Miss Super Afraid of Everything, would stay for the class? That didn't make any sense.

"Obviously," Rafael said. "I was just getting warmed up."

"I don't know," said the Human Orange. "The class is really high intensity. It's geared toward adults who've had a lot of experience. And, of course, children of the instructor, who've grown up around this type of active lifestyle." She beamed at Viv.

"Please, ma'am. We'll go slow and take it easy. And no injuries for us, promise." That could not possibly be Rafael's voice, begging like he was dying to stay up for five more minutes at night. And did he have to mention injuries? My leg throbbed like it wanted to remind me that there was totally going to be a bruise there soon.

"Well, I guess it's okay, just this once. Take it easy, though. And I'll need you to text your parents and make sure it's okay, and I'll need to e-mail them a waiver to sign electronically."

I watched Kaya. She smiled, but her bubble said exactly what I suspected: *Stay. Calm. Do. Not. Freak. Out.*

She didn't really want to stay for the class. As her best friend and the person who had brought her here in the first place, I knew I should help her escape somehow, but a weird part of me felt kinda smug, like, *Ha ha on you, that's what you get for saying you wanted to stay.* What was *wrong* with me? I was supposed to look out for her in scary situations, but all I wanted to do was leave.

Ms. Wolfson looked at me again. "I don't really feel like spin class anymore," she said. "I'm actually kind of hungry. I could go for some breakfast for dinner, if you'd care to join me for an early dinner."

Her bubble said, *I feel so sorry for Sophie,* but maybe I felt sorry for me, too, so I nodded and followed her out, right as the lights went off in the room and loud music started thumping. Out of the corner of my eyes I could see flashes of neon red, green, and blue lights. I looked back and saw circles of the colors swirling together on the ceiling, crashing into each other like they were colorful bumper cars. There was the disco ball I'd been looking for, finally—only there were more like seven thousand of them all going at once. There was no way Kaya would be into this. I didn't look back, but I bet she was staring at the door, wondering if it was too late to catch up to us.

My brain spun as Ms. Wolfson and I walked through the lobby, and I don't mean the kind of spinning as on those dumb stationary bikes. It was really no big deal that Rafael wanted to stay and Kaya sorta kinda wanted to stay and I didn't want to stay one bit. We didn't have to love all the same things. Or be good at all the same things. And this was much different than riding a real bike, anyway. And I was a great swimmer, so there was always that. Even if I was bad at bikes, I could probably still win the race if I swam fast enough to make up for it. And somehow figured out how to run.

I knew all of this, and I knew that I wanted pancakes way more than I wanted more traumatic exercise (and more time with Viv Carlson), so I should have been happy.

But as I slipped on my jacket and pushed through the gym's heavy door with Ms. Wolfson by my side, I wasn't happy at all.

15

THE TOUGH EAT PANCAKES

I WASN'T HUNGRY EITHER, AS IT TURNED OUT. THAT WAS weird. I was always hungry. Even when I was sick or tired or cranky, food was always good. Especially pancake food.

I kept picking up pieces and putting them back down, then scooting them around my plate with my fork to make it look like I had eaten a lot more than I actually had. It was a trick Mom and I came up with once when she was going out with this guy named Torin who was really good at playing drums and drawing funny pictures of animals sticking their tongues out but not so good at cooking or acting like an adult.

I giggled a little, thinking about him. He always wanted us to come over so he could cook for us, and it was super nice of him, but it was really, really, really bad food. Always. But it was still fun. Mom and I would have silent competitions to see who could make the funniest shape or design out of their dinner, and we'd share looks across the table like "Look, I turned my mashed potato–like things into the Eiffel Tower!" Then we'd go home and order a pizza and spicy garlic knots.

"At least he tried," Mom would say. "It's still probably better than what I'd make!" And then we'd laugh, because we knew it was true.

Torin never understood our looks, or the fact that we were making them because his mashed potatoes were not even close to being mashed, or potatoes. Maybe that was why he and Mom broke up, but I think it might have had more to do with that day when we realized that the reason Torin was so talented at drums and animal pictures was because he worked on both of them all day instead of going to a job. Pratik's new job meant that he was going to be off working overseas or whatever. He'd probably go to his job way too much, but Torin didn't go at all. Mom and I needed someone in the middle, maybe, who went just enough.

"Look, I turned my pancakes into a snowman!" I pointed to my plate. I had lined the three of them up so the biggest one was on the bottom and so on, and I'd made a face out of my chocolate chips.

Maybe I totally stunk at spinning, but I could make a pancake snowman like nobody's business.

"That's nice," said Ms. Wolfson, with a fake smile that reminded me a little bit of Viv's. Maybe you shouldn't brag to the person paying for your pancakes about how you're turning them into something else and not eating them, I realized a little too late.

"But, um, yeah. They're really good, though. Thanks, Ms. Wolfson." I made myself chop off some of the snowman's belly and forced it to my lips. It didn't taste bad or anything. It just didn't taste like much at all.

"For pancakes that are so good, you're hardly touching them. Aside from turning them into a snow sculpture." A smile tugged at the corners of her mouth, even though her voice sounded serious.

"Sorry. I guess I'm not that hungry. I mean, I am hungry. I'm always hungry. I just don't feel like eating. So it's sorta confusing."

"It's okay that you fell off that bike, you know. No matter what my spin teacher thought about it. No one's perfect. And you know what they say—when the going gets tough, the tough eat their pancakes."

A small giggle escaped my mouth. That was so not what they said, whoever they were, but I liked this new expression better than whatever the original was.

"What were you and your friends doing there, anyway?"

She wasn't asking in a mean way or an I'm-trying-to-get-you-in-trouble way. It seemed like she just really wanted to know. And she liked breakfast food almost as much as Mom and me, so she was probably an okay person to tell.

"We were practicing for this mini-triathlon we're doing in April," I said. "My mom doesn't really care. But she will." I picked at my pancakes some more.

"She's been unhappy," Ms. Wolfson said, sorta like she was asking me even though she already knew the answer. "It's not going well with Neighbor Boy."

"They broke up a while ago," I said.

"Oh, I'm sorry to hear that." Ms. Wolfson raised her eyebrows and studied me over her plate. "I haven't seen your mom in the lobby much lately. Guess that explains it, huh? Although she always looks very nice when I see her. You'd never know anything was wrong."

"Well, come upstairs at night sometime," I said with a groan. Almost instantly I felt terrible, like I'd kicked myself in the gut or something. I shouldn't spill the truth about Mom like that. She'd never told any of my secrets in the whole twelve years I'd known her, and here I'd just blabbed hers without a second thought.

"You know, a lot of times people only show off their highlights," Ms. Wolfson said. She took a huge sip of her chocolate milk and blew a few bubbles in it with her straw. "People show you what they want you to see and believe. Your mom might want everyone to think she's one thing, but then when she's in her home with the person she loves . . ." she nodded at me, "she feels safe enough to be something else."

I blew bubbles in my chocolate milk, too, as I thought that over. First things first, she was onto something. Why had I not blown bubbles in milk in so long? It was way fun. Second, that made a lot of sense.

"Well, I'm . . ." I stopped. I was about to say that I was tired of being the one she loved, the one she was her real self around. But that was by far the meanest thing I could ever say. It was bad enough to think it.

"Anyway, your mom is going to be just fine," Ms. Wolfson continued.

"How do you know that?"

"Because. Wolfson women are not doormats. Which is how I know you're going to be just fine, too. With your friends, with your race, everything." She folded her hands in her lap.

I folded my hands in my lap, too.

"Doormats?" I asked. Mom and I had a doormat. It was blue and it said HI. I'M MAT. I didn't think about

Mat much; I just stepped on him anytime I went in or out of our condo. And I had no idea what he had to do with anything we were talking about right now.

"I know we're not related, but since we're neighbors who have shared cocoa and cribbage, I hereby consider you a Wolfson woman. Your mom, too, of course. And Wolfson women don't let anyone make them feel that they can be walked on. No one treats us that way. Not stationary bikes. Not races. Not boyfriends or ex-boyfriends or anybody else."

I smiled. Now I was thinking about Mat a lot. Even though he wasn't real or anything—poor guy. Mom and I stepped on him with muddy shoes. Snowy shoes. Shoes that had stepped in mushy dog poop. And he just had to take it.

But we didn't.

I smiled, took a bite of pancake, and looked around the diner. In the corner, a bubble had popped up over a guy's head. He looked like a regular guy. Maybe a little scraggly (kinda like Pratik when he had all his face hair going on), but regular, like he could be somebody's dad. He was taking a sip out of a coffee cup and staring into space. The bubble said, *I haven't eaten in two days.*

I looked down at what was left of my pancake snowman, feeling like a terrible person. Here I was, messing around instead of eating, basically wasting the awesome food in front of me, getting a little confused by the person I was talking to, but at least I *had* someone to talk to, and meanwhile there was someone in the same room who hadn't eaten in forty-eight hours. My stomach rumbled just thinking about having to survive something like that.

Ms. Wolfson followed my gaze across the room. Then she said, "Let's get that man something to eat, shall we?" She waved and our waitress came over. "Can you add another order of pancakes to my tab? And please take it to the man in the corner, but don't tell him who sent it." The waitress nodded and went away.

Meanwhile, my eyes were almost popping out of my head. How did Ms. Wolfson know about that guy? She looked my way and winked.

Holy chocolate pancakes. Could it be? Ms. Wolfson knew about my bubbles. It was the only possible explanation. Or, even freakier yet . . . she saw them, too.

16
WRISTBANDS

OBVIOUSLY SHE DIDN'T WANT ME TO KNOW FOR SOME reason, since she wasn't coming right out and telling me. I wished a bubble would appear over her head, something that would tell me what to do. Maybe a nice *Yeah, it's okay, ask me* or an *Ignore it and ask me about cribbage strategies.* Anything would be better than what I had to work with now.

"It's been about forty-five minutes," Ms. Wolfson said after she paid the bill. "Let's run back to the gym and grab your friends."

I groaned inside my head. I kinda figured they'd get home on their own; none of us lived far, so they could walk together. I didn't really want to see them and talk about my super embarrassing fall. I wasn't a doormat or anything. I could act tough. But I couldn't make the fall—or the bruise—disappear. Would Rafael still think I was awesome after something like that?

The thought of Kaya and Rafael walking together without me made the pancakes churn around and around in my stomach. It was fine that they were in Dumb Fake Biking Class of Doom together because they couldn't really talk to each other and do that at the same time. Unless they were so incredibly talented that they could. Which, at this point, wouldn't surprise me that much.

"Okay." I zipped up my jacket. "Yeah, let's go back and get them."

As we walked toward the door, we passed the guy who hadn't eaten in two days, who now had a giant steaming hot breakfast-for-dinner plate in front of him. He looked up at us and grinned from ear to ear, though he didn't know who had given him the meal. He was smiling at everyone who passed by, not just us. And he was gobbling it down like they were the best pancakes he'd ever eaten in his life.

By the time we got to the gym, I was a little happier. It was cool that we'd used that bubble to help someone. But what wasn't cool was the way Kaya, Rafael, and Viv were standing in front of the gym all smiley, talking and giggling and looking at each other like no one else on the whole planet existed.

My heart felt like it'd dropped all the way from the

top of Mount Fitz Roy, that ridiculously tall mountain in Argentina.

"Hi, guys," I said. My voice came out in a whisper, so no one heard. But they still had eyes, didn't they? They should be able to see me standing right next to them. Only if they did see me, no one said a thing.

"Hi," I tried again, a little louder.

"Sophie!" Rafael turned to me. Kaya and Viv were still talking to each other. What was so important that they couldn't stop for a second to care that I was back?

"You should've stayed," Rafael shouted to me. "It was amazing! We spun to this awesome playlist, and there were flashing lights, and it was like the coolest dance party ever, only on bikes!"

"You don't have to yell," I said. "I'm right here."

At least he was talking to me, though, even if he was doing it way too loudly.

"Sorry! We had to scream at the top of our lungs to talk to each other in there. It was the best thing ever!"

Kaya and Viv's Super Important Chat finally ended, and Kaya and Rafael said bye to Viv in this super long, dramatic, goodbye-forever kind of way, like it was going to be twelve years before they saw her again, not twelve hours.

When Ms. Wolfson, Rafael, Kaya, and I got outside, Kaya started skipping down the sidewalk. Skipping down the sidewalk! Obviously she was happy about something, which was good. But I'd missed it, whatever it was. I'd ditched them when they were doing this for me. It wasn't her fault she was amazing at it and I stank.

I picked up my pace. There was a bubble forming over Kaya's head, bouncing right along with her with each skip.

This is crazy, it said.

I took a couple steps back as the bubble disappeared. I guess what it said made sense, sorta. Kaya had done totally new things tonight, and it was a huge deal for her. She was probably completely freaking out. She probably *had* freaked out, during the class. And I hadn't been there for her. But if she was freaking out, why did she seem so happy?

"Rafael, tell them the best part," Kaya yelled over her shoulder in a loud singsongy voice.

Kaya never used a loud singsongy voice. We made fun of loud singsongy voices.

"Viv's mom thought we did such a good job that she gave us these fancy wristbands! We are such legit biker people now it's unbelievable." He held out his arm and rolled his jacket sleeve up so I could see the thick black band around his wrist. "She even gave us a special pass so we can go to another class even though we're so young."

"Cool," I squeaked.

Kaya turned and skipped back so she was with the rest of us instead of a hundred miles ahead. Her hair was down, blowing around in the breeze, and the smile on her face was gigantic. She looked like she could rocket right off the ground and fly the rest of the way home. I should have been excited for her, but if there were a bubble over my head it'd say *Not excited for Kaya. Terrible friend. Should be forced to fall off a fake bike a hundred times over.*

"I asked if we could have one for you, too," she said to me. "But she didn't think that was a good idea. Sorry." Then she slowed down a lot and said quietly, "Viv isn't going to replace you or anything. You're still our best friend."

My already messed-up heart felt like somebody had poked it with William Wallace's famous sword from the Wars of Scottish Independence in the thirteenth century. It was just . . . no. Viv replacing me—what if *that* was her project?

No. It couldn't be. But wasn't it kinda weird that she kept looking at Kaya and me at school and talking to us in the hall and now she was doing our triathlon *and* inviting my friends to all these spin classes? It was almost like Viv was trying to steal them.

It was a lot like that, actually.

A thick lump formed in my throat and I couldn't swallow it no matter how hard I tried. Sure, Kaya said Viv wouldn't replace me, but that was now. What about after their next spin class? What if Viv was amazing at everything and I continued to be terrible? What if Rafael started liking Viv more than he liked me? What if he already did?

I looked up at the dark sky, waiting, watching, hoping. *Come on, Rafael's bubble.* But it didn't come. Ms. Wolfson started walking next to me and talking to me about cribbage, but I couldn't pay attention. All I could see were Rafael's and Kaya's backs as they walked up ahead, talking about spinning or Viv or whatever, going on without me.

17

HIGHLIGHTS

AFTER WE DROPPED KAYA AND RAFAEL OFF AND SAID good night, I went upstairs to find Mom on the couch poring over *Weaver's Weekly*. She looked up at me with sad eyes. She didn't say "How was practice?" or "Why were you gone for so long?" or "Did you eat pancakes without me?" She didn't say anything at all.

So I said, "I fell off a stationary bike," because why not?

"Oh yeah?" She motioned for me to join her on the couch. I plopped down and snuggled up beside her, stealing some of the wool blanket to cover my tired, achy, bruise-y legs.

Neither of us said anything for a minute. I could tell Mom was trying to act normal, but there was nothing normal about dabbing at her eyes every two seconds for what felt like the zillionth day in a row.

She sniffled and wrapped an arm around my shoulders. "So are you okay? From your fall?"

"Yeah. I'm gonna have a major bruise though."

"And how are your, um, bubble things doing?"

I frowned. We both knew I couldn't really talk to her about it. She was like the Colossus of Rhodes (one of the tallest, coolest statues of the ancient world) during the earthquake of 226 B.C.: falling apart, piece by piece.

"They're still there. They're okay. I'm dealing."

Neither of us said anything for a minute. Mom gave me a little more of the blanket.

"I haven't been that great of a mom lately," she said. "I'm sorry, Sophie. I'm just so . . ." Her voice cracked and trailed off.

"It's okay. I know it won't last forever." I gave the piece of blanket back to her.

Know was kind of a strong word, based on how everything had gone today. I wasn't going to be a doormat about it—I'd keep trying—but maybe the super awesome triathlon scene in my head wasn't going to happen. Especially if I couldn't even stay on the dumb bike. How was I going to win the race—or even do the race—if I couldn't stay on the dumb bike?

Mom reached out and tucked one of my curls behind my ear, something she hadn't done in ages.

"No, it won't last forever," she said. Then her bubble added, *But I really don't know that for a fact.*

• • •

Mom must've done all her weird whimper noises while I was out, because it seemed like she didn't have any left for bedtime, so that was good. I stayed up till way past droopy-eyelid time just to make sure she got in bed okay and didn't cry.

While I stayed awake, I decided to catch up on my Internet stalking. Mom and I shared the computer, but she let me keep it in my room. I went to Pratik's online profile first and noticed that he had a whole bunch of new friends. They looked awesome. Their pictures showed them dancing in fancy outfits, smiling around a campfire, and making funny faces with cute little kids. I wondered if that was what their lives were really like, or if they were just showing off the highlights, like Ms. Wolfson said. Ms. Wolfson was talking about real people, not about online profiles, but was there really that much of a difference? After all, your profile was supposed to show your life.

A little red icon popped up, saying that I had two new updates. I clicked on it.

Rafael Garcia is now friends with Viv Carlson, it said.

Kaya Lewis is now friends with Viv Carlson

Everyone is now friends with Viv Carlson

Probably even Pratik is now friends with Viv Carlson

Because seriously, everyone is now friends with Viv Carlson

Except you, Sophie

So that's awkward

It didn't really say those last few things, but that's what it felt like. I saw the words so clearly in my mind that it was kind of a surprise not to see them on the website.

I knew there wouldn't be anything there, but I clicked on my friend requests just in case. The notification didn't always come up, so I could totally have had one that just wasn't showing up because sometimes the Internet was a mystery.

But I didn't have a friend request. Not one. Not even from some random old-person relative or a stranger who was actually a spammy robot whose friendship you're supposed to reject.

I sighed and shut our computer down. There was no point in staring at the little "0 requests" sad-face-icon guy. And there was the fact that I didn't want to be friends with Viv anyway.

But everybody else did, all of a sudden. Viv with her

orange mom and her fancy spinning leggings and her triathloning "for fun" and her risk project that was "more challenging," like ours was the easiest thing on the planet.

Well, we'd see how easy she thought it was when I won first place.

I rubbed my bruise-free leg so it would be in tip-top shape for our next practice. Yeah, Viv was perfect in pretty much every way. But, I wondered, a small smile inching onto my face—could she swim?

18

BUBBLES ARE UPON US

"HOW ARE YOU?"

"Fine, how are you?"

No answer. Dr. Llama just sat there looking at me and not talking. Maybe he wanted to go back to sleep. I did. It was way hard being up this early on a Saturday, even for a morning person like me.

"I fell off a bike that wasn't moving," I told him. I was seriously going to fall asleep in this chair (which was a teeny bit comfier than it was last time) if we didn't start talking soon. "Ridiculous, right? My bruise is gigantic. Like I have more bruise than leg."

He didn't say anything, so I kept talking. I talked about the risk project, about agreeing to do the triathlon, about how I hoped that doing it and winning it would bring Mom (and me) back to normal. The words just kept spilling out of me. I told him about feeling weird that Kaya and Rafael were awesome at biking and had spent extra time together without me, but how I couldn't be mad at them because they were doing the race for me; they were trying to help me even though now it sorta seemed like they were more interested in spinning and wristbands than they were in making sure I was myself again.

And then I talked more about the bikes.

"Normal bikes aren't like that. It was *such* a weird bike. That's probably why I fell off it."

Dr. Llama frowned. I bet he could tell that I had about as much athletic ability as the paintings on his wall.

"I don't know." I slumped down in the chair and silently promised myself that I'd stop talking soon. "Maybe it's because the bubbles are interrupting my concentration. Sometimes I wish they would go away, but a lot of the time I wish they said more. So basically I'm a big bundle of confusion."

There. I zipped my lips shut. I was done.

"The end," I added.

Dr. Llama didn't say anything for a few minutes. He just looked at me, and looked at the paintings, and then he finally asked in his calm, quiet, llama-y voice, "Did you ever hear the story about the king?"

I un-slumped myself from the chair as fast as I could.

"Which one? King Henry VII of England? Louis XIII of France? Felipe or Ferdinand of Spain?"

He laughed. "No king in particular. Take your pick."

"Wait, why not a queen?"

He scratched his chin. "I'm not sure. It could be a queen."

Queens did cool queenly things throughout history, but kings usually got all the credit.

"Let's make it a queen," I said.

Dr. Llama smiled. "So this queen," he said. "She decided she would go to war. The troops from the other side surrounded her castle, and the knight came to alert her that they were there. *But I don't want to go to war,* the queen exclaimed. *But, madam,* said the knight. *It's too late. War is upon us.*"

He looked me in the eyes. "War is upon us," he repeated. "Whether you like them or not, you've been given these bubbles. What you do next is up to you. But the bubbles are upon you. And so is this triathlon. Everything you've just described is upon you. Some of it you chose. Some of it you didn't. But it doesn't matter, because it's all happening."

He was right. There wasn't really a choice to make. I couldn't decide if I wanted the bubbles or not, because they were already here. I had them. They were mine.

"What did the queen do next?" I asked.

But Dr. Llama didn't answer. He smiled, stood up, and opened the door, pointing to the room where Mom was waiting.

We were done for the day.

19

NOODLING & OTHER NON-DROWNING ACTIVITIES

I THOUGHT ABOUT QUEENS THE WHOLE BUS RIDE FROM therapy. One of the coolest queens in history was Eleanor of Aquitaine. She didn't like some of the stuff her husband was doing, and neither did her kids, so she supported them when they wanted to start a big revolt in 1173. Her husband was so mad about it that he locked her away in jail. She only got to be free because eventually he died and one of their kids took over and let her out.

A whole lot of stuff was upon Eleanor of Aquitaine. But if she could deal with a revolt and heavy-duty jail time, then I could deal with some bubbles and some sports. And this practice would be easy, anyway. It was just swimming. I could definitely swim.

When Mom and I got home, I grabbed my swimming

suit and headed to the gym to meet Kaya and Rafael. This time, we changed in the fancy locker rooms with ginormous lockers and rooms filled with steam, and once we met up again, we walked in the opposite direction of the terrible Spin Room of Doom, which was good news. I did not need to see those phony bikes again for a long, long time (or ever, if I could help it).

We passed a sign that said INDOOR POOL and turned down a winding hallway that reeked of chlorine. To me, it smelled pretty gross, but to Kaya, I could tell, it smelled like her worst fear come true.

"I can't do it." She plopped down right there on the floor in the middle of the hallway. Then she took her towel and put it on top of her head like she wanted it to make her invisible.

"Kaya, we can still see you." I sat down beside her and grabbed the towel from her head. "And now we can really see you!"

Even though the area was warm, she was totally shaking from head to toe. Seeing her all shaky made *me* feel all shaky, and I wasn't even scared. Or maybe I was. She was doing this because of me, and I had to make sure it went well, even if maybe she'd rather be here with Viv Carlson instead of me.

"Kaya, you can totally do this," I said.

I can't, her bubble argued.

What if she couldn't do this?

"You are perfectly healthy," I continued. "You are smart. You do not fall off stationary bikes."

What if *I* couldn't do this?

I tried to make my voice come out normal, but it was as wobbly as my body had been before I fell off that dumb bike.

"We'll be there for you the whole entire time," Rafael said. "Plus, there are noodles."

"Noodles?" Kaya made a face like he'd actually said *tarantulas*.

"Yes, noodles," Rafael said. "They're so great for noodling! And other non-drowning activities."

Kaya took a big, long breath, and looked at both of us looking at her.

"Okay."

"Okay," I agreed.

"This is the part where you get up and we go swim," Rafael told her, but she didn't budge.

"No one's going to let you drown," he said. "Remember the other night after spin class, before Sophie got there, when we were by the vending machines and you almost tripped over your shoelace and went flying?"

They hung out by the vending machines after spin class?

"Yeah, I remember." Kaya smiled.

"And what happened?" Rafael asked.

"I didn't."

Was it just my imagination, or were her eyes extra twinkly all of a sudden?

"And why not?"

"Because you caught me and made me stand still, and Viv tied my shoe for me so I could have my hands free to tell the vending machine what I wanted before it forgot I had put money in."

She stood up.

"Exactly. So, it'll be like that. Only no laces in the way!"

Now Kaya was grinning. Rafael linked his arm through hers and practically pulled her down the hall.

I trailed after them with my arms crossed over my chest. The hallway was pretty narrow, but there was totally room for three people to all link arms and walk together. So why hadn't anybody grabbed on to me? If Viv Carlson was here, would they have grabbed on to her?

It was great that Kaya was about to go swim and face one of her biggest fears, and I was sorta excited to get in the pool and help her. But if that was true, then why did I feel like I was sinking?

20

THE POOL

WE WENT INTO THE POOL AREA AND LOOKED AROUND.
Aside from a small group of kids and a lady in a fancy
swim cap, it was pretty empty.

"So . . . what now?" Kaya twirled a huge chunk of
hair.

"Cannonball?"

We both shot Rafael a look.

"Or we could sit." He pointed to the edge near the
shallow end.

Kaya took a deep breath. "Sitting would be good."

So we plopped down by the shallow end of the pool,
the three of us in a row with me in the middle. I breathed
in that weird/awesome Rafael-y smell, feeling like a major
creeper. But there was something calming about it. Kaya

needed jokes to relax, and I needed to creepily inhale the scent of a boy who probably needed to start wearing deodorant.

I looked at Kaya on my other side. Something was different about her today but I couldn't figure out what it was, aside from her new online friendship with Viv and her hilarious shoe-tying/going-flying story from after spin class. It wasn't that. It was something in the way she looked. Her hair was long and flowy like normal, and her braces were still there, still the same light pink color they'd been all week. So what was it?

Aha! I knew what it was. Kaya didn't have leg hair anymore.

It might have been a weird thing to notice. Maybe it was strange to be looking at my best friend's legs this closely, or at all. But that's what was different. I checked her arms, just to make sure. Even in the dim pool lights, I could see the thin black lines sprouting every which way. But there weren't any on her legs. They looked shinier and smoother than the kitchen table right after we cleaned up from dinner.

I glanced down at my own short, stubby legs. I knew I was shorter than both of them, but my legs were seriously little compared to Kaya's, which were long and thin and dipped way far down into the pool.

Plus, mine had clumps—clumps!—of brownish hair going in every direction. Ew! How had I never noticed this before? My legs were so gross. No wonder Kaya was better at spinning; she didn't have like a thousand pounds of leg hair weighing her down. And no wonder Rafael was looking at her like she'd been declared an Olympic swimmer. She was turning into a supermodel while I was turning into a grizzly bear.

"Well, this has been some great sitting," Rafael said after we'd all been quiet for a few minutes. "Cannonball time?"

He was definitely getting antsy, and so was Kaya. Maybe I was, too. But all I knew about what to do next was that it probably shouldn't be a cannonball if we didn't want to send Kaya running away screaming.

"Maybe we should practice kicking," I said. "That's a pretty important part of swimming."

"Yeah!" Kaya shot Rafael a humongous grin, like it had been his idea and not mine. I made a face, but no one seemed to notice.

We all started kicking our feet up and down, softly at first, then harder and harder. Maybe too hard. Or maybe that was just me.

"Slow down," Kaya told me.

"Yeah, seriously, Sophie. Are you trying to get the

whole pool's worth of water up my nose?" Rafael sounded like he was joking, but his face looked annoyed.

I didn't mean to kick a whole pool of water up his nose. I just wanted him to look at me in that same you're-cool-and-totally-not-a-grizzly-bear way he was still looking at Kaya the Future Supermodel and All-Around Perfect Athlete.

Just like her legs, Kaya's kicks were perfectly smooth. She kept her legs straight and carefully lifted them up and back down, sending the perfect amount of ripple through the water. It was so unfair, so I kicked harder.

"So, wait, I'm confused. Are we just warming up our feet right now, or are we trying to use them as weapons of mass de-splashitude?" Rafael asked.

My face burned and tears poked at the sides of my eyes. Even when I slowed my feet down, they weren't working right. One of them turned sideways a little, so I was accidentally sending water in Rafael's direction even though I wasn't trying to anymore. The other one was off in its own foot world. Instead of bopping up and down it rotated from side to side, almost making circles and not making kicks at all. Spinning and standing up and down on the pedals had ten zillion things to remember, but kicking only had one basic rule: kick. And I still couldn't do it.

"Okay, enough kicking," Rafael decided. "We're

getting in the water. Prepare yourselves. It's cannonball time!"

He got up, walked to the deep end, and jumped in. Kaya went over to the stairs at the shallow end and very carefully dipped in one toe at a time, even though she'd had her feet in the water only a minute ago. I stayed sitting by the edge and slowly wriggled my body down from the wall into the pool. The water only came up to my belly button, so I bobbed under. The last time I swam, when we were in Florida visiting my grandparents a couple years ago, Mom and I held hands and took a running leap right off the dock and into the ocean. It was freezing. I had never been so cold in my whole life. But we were both laughing when we floated to the top.

I sure didn't feel like laughing now.

I poked my head out of the water and whipped my hair around me. Curls were stuck to my neck, my shoulders, my cheeks, everywhere. I blinked the extra water out of my eyes and tried to see where everybody was. Oh . . . Kaya and Rafael were both in the shallow end now, splashing each other and laughing like it was the most fun they'd ever had.

That was . . . interesting.

I made my way over and tried to make myself smile,

like I was in on the fun, not just standing there awkwardly watching it. My friend who was afraid of swimming was in the pool and she was almost swimming. She was really happy! She wasn't freaking out or drowning or being mad at me for sorta being the reason she was in this situation in the first place. I should've been happy, too. And I was . . . sort of.

But also, sort of not.

"Isn't this great?" Rafael stopped splashing and karate-chopped the water. "We own you, pool. You are no match for Kaya the Swimming Beast! There isn't even any noodling happening here. Do you realize that, Kaya? You. Are. Not. Noodling!"

Neither am I, I wanted to tell him. But I already knew how to swim, so that wasn't a big deal. This was about Kaya. He was just being a nice, encouraging friend. It was one of the things I liked most about him.

I just didn't like it as much right this second.

But maybe I could remind him I was still here. I didn't have anything to say about noodles, but I still had good ideas.

"Maybe we should warm up our arms," I told them. I waved one arm over my shoulder to demonstrate, and then the other.

Good thinking, Sophie, said Rafael's bubble. I didn't

know why he didn't say it out loud, but it didn't matter. All that mattered was that they totally still needed me, and they were happy the three of us were doing this together.

Kaya rolled her right arm over her shoulder in a way so graceful it'd make a real ballerina jealous. For someone who was scared of everything, she was sure good at everything.

Meanwhile, my arms might as well have been octopus tentacles. They floundered all over the place; it was like I had no control of them whatsoever, even though they were attached to me. Why was I so terrible at this arm thing? And the kicking thing? And the biking thing? And *all the things*? I stared out toward the deep end, afraid to look at my friends because I might start crying.

"Let's stop warming up our arms," I called over my shoulder.

But they didn't stop warming up their arms.

They were laughing again, at something I hadn't caught. And their arms were going back and forth a million miles a minute and it was like they didn't have to put any effort into it at all. Why was it so hard for me but easy for them? And how was I going to remind Mom how great races were when I was awful at everything?

How was I going to remind her how to have fun when there wasn't anything fun about this?

"I'm going to take a break," I said, and got out and grabbed my towel without looking at anyone. Not like anyone would be that concerned anyway.

As I left, though, I glanced back over my shoulder. Kaya and Rafael were splashing around and looking at each other and laughing their heads off.

I walked away, and they didn't even notice.

21
STEAM

I STORMED THROUGH THE HALLWAY WE'D COME FROM. IT still smelled gross, like chlorine, only now it was annoying. That smell was gross. Pools were gross. Everything was gross.

I went into the locker room and thought about what to do next. Going home didn't sound so great, but I definitely didn't want to go back to the pool.

That didn't leave a whole lot of choices.

Then I remembered the giant room of steam. I'd never been in a room made out of steam before. That could be fun. I glanced at the sign—18+, it said. Well, I was almost eighteen. There were only six short years to go. That was like nothing. And if I just went in for a minute, that didn't really count anyway.

I looked to my left and to my right, in case there

were Steam Room Police standing by. I didn't see any, so I cracked the door open and slipped inside.

"Hello?"

The steam was so cloudy and heavy that you couldn't see your own arm, let alone any other people.

A voice laughed through the fog. "You sound like a newbie. Take a seat. Watch out for corners. The bench is closer than you think it is."

"Ow!" As she talked, my knee found the bench and I winced. That was definitely going to be another bruise. Now not only had I been beaten up by a fake bike, I had also gotten beat up by a bench. Awesome.

Okay, well, this had been an interesting experiment. I'd have to tell Kaya about it if I could pry her away from Rafael and Viv and her hairless legs and bazillion new skills long enough to talk to me.

Thinking about talking to Kaya—and going back to the pool—made my stomach hurt. But I had to go back to the pool. I had to get better at swimming. What was I even doing? I had to win this race for Mom, and I was totally wasting my practice time. You couldn't just ditch something if it got hard. If Thomas Edison gave up when things got tough, we probably wouldn't have light bulbs. (Seriously, the guy failed over *a thousand times* before it finally worked.) But Thomas Edison was actually good at inventing and knew things about electricity. And clearly I knew nothing about sports . . . or my best friends.

I was about to push open the door when I noticed something that made my steamed-up eyes almost pop out of my head. How was this even possible in such a hazy place? There were bubbles everywhere. Well, I assumed they were bubbles. All I could really see were the words floating above me in the steamy air. Since I couldn't see any people, I couldn't tell which bubbles went to who. Or who the people even were. Or why I cared, to be honest. But the words were practically swimming in my face, begging to be read. I couldn't ignore them. That would be rude. And like Mom always used to say when she took me to the public library— Adventurous Girls read.

Don't. Cry.

I hope I don't get caught.

What was I thinking?

Where did the time go?

I should have figured it out sooner.

I can't take it anymore.

There were more, but I didn't want to read them. They were too depressing, and what had been a sad kind of day was turning into the biggest bummer of a day since the vending machine with all the best junk food got taken out of the cafeteria.

The air in the locker room was freezing. I wrapped myself in a second towel, then a third. I plopped down on the bench I'd sat on before and let the towels soak up all the steam and sweat escaping from my skin.

I had to go back to the pool. For Mom, even though she didn't actually know I wanted to win so bad because of her. For Kaya, even though she wasn't that scared anymore. For Rafael, who wanted to hang out with me, even though he was kinda acting like he didn't. And maybe for me, too. For Adventurous Girl Sophie or Regular Sophie or whoever the heck I was.

I sighed. Maybe there were no happy bubbles because there were no happy people. Everywhere I went—the steam room, the sidewalks, school—people were worried or stressed about something, and if they weren't that, they were sad. They wished things had never happened or had happened differently. And it wasn't only the strangers. It was people I knew, too. Like Kaya and Rafael. Even though they were having fun now, it didn't mean they would have fun forever. Even if the triathlon somehow worked out the way I wanted it to, maybe there would always be something bringing me—and Mom—down.

If everyone regretted everything, I wondered as I got up, then what was the point of doing anything at all?

22
SWIMMING (OR SOMETHING)

"I'M SWIMMING AND I'M NOT THAT SCARED!" I COULD hear Kaya's excited voice all the way from the Chlorine Hall. You could probably hear it on Mars, too.

Even though I was upset, I had to smile when I got back into the pool area. She *was* swimming. And grouchy as I was, I had to admit, it was pretty cool, even though I hadn't helped her not be afraid like I was supposed to.

I clapped my hands and cheered. "Woo! Go, Kaya!"

She stopped, stood up (she was still in the shallow end), and waved.

"Where were you?" she asked, once she was done coughing up the gallon of water that had ended up in her mouth.

"I just went to get a drink," I said. My face felt hot. I didn't like lying to her, or to anyone, but it was probably better to keep my steam room adventure to myself. Especially the part about seeing all the bubbles. And getting yet another ridiculous injury.

Kaya waded over to the stairs.

"I'm taking five. Want a break, Rafael?"

"No way," he said. "Breaks are for the weak! Sorry," he added when he saw my face. "Not like, weak weak. Just like . . . swimming rules!" He dove under and waved his feet back and forth in the air. Then he pretended that his left foot was chasing his right. Kaya and I giggled. It was hard to stay mad at someone who'd put on an underwater puppet show for you with his feet.

Kaya and I pulled towels around our legs and sat on some lounge chairs near the door. If I closed my eyes, I could pretend I was on a warm beach somewhere, a place where best friends were equally good at things and didn't become friends with people like Viv Carlson. A place where moms were happy and stationary bikes and steam and weird bubbles didn't exist. I let out a long, slow breath and fully let myself pretend I was there. My fake beach was almost better than visiting Colonial Williamsburg with Mom a couple years ago, which was basically the best thing ever.

Kaya poked me in the stomach, making my dream place totally disappear, and making me jump about a thousand feet into the air.

"Since when are you so ticklish?" she asked.

Since when are you getting rid of your leg hair? I wanted to say, but it came out as a shrug instead.

"So, how are you doing?" she asked.

"Fine, how are you? You're a great swimmer."

No thanks to me, I added in my head.

"Thanks! It's so much better than I remembered. Are you sure everything's okay? You were gone for a long time." She twisted some hair around her fingers.

I chewed on the inside of my cheek. What should I tell her? Everything I thought of sounded dumb. Plus, I definitely couldn't tell her how I was feeling left out with her and Rafael, since Rafael was right by us in the pool. I definitely *definitely* couldn't tell her about the fluttery heart feelings I had when Rafael was nearby— the kinds of feelings she was basically squashing with her crazy athletic talents and snazzy hairless legs. So I said nothing and stared out into the pool, pretending I was super interested in watching the lady with the bright pink swim cap do laps back and forth.

Kaya watched me. "Is it about those bubbles you told me about before? Is that why you're acting weird? Have you seen more of them?"

Like you wouldn't believe, I wanted to say, but I bit my tongue instead. Yeah, I wanted to tell her all the details, but what if she went blabbing to Rafael or Viv?

"I've seen some," I said. "Mostly kinda depressing stuff. So yeah, that could be why I'm acting weird."

"Oh."

"Yeah."

That's when I noticed that one was forming right above her head. The little dots showed up so slowly it was like they were purposely taking forever and being dramatic.

Then the big bubble formed, then the words. I tried so hard to keep eye contact with Kaya. If anyone would notice that I was actually looking above her head, trying to make out the little words that appeared one at a time, it would be her. And I had a feeling that this was going to be something I was going to want to keep to myself.

My life is amazing! I can swim and Rafael is my boyfriend!

I snapped my mouth shut, stood up, and then everything went black.

23

SPLAT

I WAS PRETTY SURE MY ARMPIT WAS BROKEN.

Can you even break an armpit?

Also, what good are they if they break?

(Actually, what good are they anyway?)

My ankle hurt, too. A lot. I bent down to rub it, but the stretch made my armpit hurt more.

Kaya and Rafael gathered around me like it was all over. *So long, Sophie,* their eyes were saying. *It was nice knowing you. Now go away already so we can concentrate on our triathlon and our new friend Viv and also going out, because apparently we do that now.*

I felt a second wave of dizziness so I leaned back in the chair. Dizziness had caused this in the first place, I was pretty sure, and I couldn't risk a second broken armpit.

"You really fell," said Kaya, as if I didn't know.

"Yeah, when you try to stand up, you're supposed to, like, stand up," said Rafael. "Not get tangled up in the chair and land all . . ." he spread his arms out and waved them like he was doing a goofy dance. "*Splat* on the ground."

I clutched my shoulder as pain shot through the inside of my armpit and sped down my side. At least it wasn't another bruise on my leg. But maybe that would have been better than a broken armpit. Where would they put a cast, anyway? And my ankle. I definitely couldn't do a triathlon with a broken ankle. Although it was kinda looking like I wouldn't be able to do one even with an ankle that worked.

The pool door creaked and two people walked in. I held my armpit and squeezed my eyes shut. Whoever the people were, I didn't want to see them and I didn't want them to see me. Closing my eyes wouldn't make me invisible, but I could pretend.

"Whoa. Now what happened?"

I knew that voice.

"Did you fall off, like, a noodle? I don't get this."

"I can take a look, if you want."

I knew that voice, too. It sounded like snootiness mixed with the color orange.

"I have a background in sports medicine," Viv's mom continued. "Were you swimming when this happened?"

I shook my head, eyes still shut.

"She was getting off the chair," Kaya told her.

I squeezed my eyes shut even tighter, like that would somehow make everybody go away. I'd rather be alone with my broken armpit and swollen ankle than be with traitor friends and people who thought my serious injuries were more entertaining than watching the world's first movie (which came out in 1888).

"I'm going to get some supplies." Viv's mom pointed at Kaya and Rafael. "You two, come with me. Vivian, stay with the patient."

I opened my eyes just in time to see a bubble appear over Viv's head. *Mom thinks I can stay alone with the patient? Maybe I could be a doctor someday. I can be anything I want!*

Ugh. I thought I would have rather gone with Viv's mom, even though I couldn't exactly move.

Viv and I stared at each other for what felt like forever.

"So . . . do you feel okay?" she finally asked.

"Delightful."

A little redness crept onto her cheeks, and she looked all around, like she was wondering what was taking everybody so long. I was wondering the same thing.

I glanced down at Viv's legs. Hairless. Of course.

"Do you want me to hold your ankle or something?" Her voice was all high and squeaky, and now her cheeks were even redder than her hair. Was Viv Carlson, master of spinning and sports and all the things ever in the universe, . . . nervous? Did she think I was going to fall off the chair again and hurt myself more and she'd have to deal with it all by herself? And if she wasn't worried about that, then what was she worried about? Maybe she knew I was onto her and her rotten project.

"No thanks."

"Are you still glad you're doing the triathlon for the project?" the Friend Stealer asked.

"Mmm-hmm."

I sat up a little straighter as I realized something: this was my chance. Maybe I could get her to admit it, to get everything out in the open. Then I could nicely tell her to go find something else to do. "Hey," I said as casually as I could, "you never told me what you're doing for your project."

She swayed back and forth on her flip-flops. "I'm . . . I'm doing something that has a lot of steps."

I should've picked something else, said her bubble.

It went away and a second one popped up. *No, I can do this project. I'm great. I'm Viv Carlson!*

"Like what kind of steps?"

"Just, like, steps, okay? It's complicated."

It sure didn't seem that complicated. It seemed like it was working exactly how she wanted it to.

Before I could say anything more, the pool door opened and Rafael, Kaya, and Viv's mom came back. Between the three of them, they were carrying a huge ice pack, a few big cushions, and what looked like a ten-thousand-pound roll of ACE bandages.

In less than a second, Viv's face went back to a normal color. She stopped rocking back and forth. If she had been nervous that I was onto her, she sure wasn't nervous anymore.

While Viv's mom hoisted my foot up over the cushions, Viv turned to Kaya and Rafael. "I was thinking of designing a custom T-shirt for the race," she said. "You know, like something bright, to stand out in the crowd. If you want, I could order some for you, too. We could put a team name on them or something, since we're basically doing the race together, right?"

"That'd be cool," Kaya said.

"We could be Team Rafael!" said Rafael.

"Ha. Um, no," Viv said. "I was thinking we could combine the first letters of our names. So be SKRV. Or VSRK. Or RKSV. Doesn't matter which one. They're all super catchy." She smiled like she was doing us a huge favor, and a bubble appeared over her head.

She's the luckiest person in the world.

She was obviously thinking about Kaya, but why? Did she know about Kaya and Rafael already? Of course she wanted a boyfriend now that more people were getting them. And wait a second; they told *her* and not me?

That was the last straw. Swollen ankle and broken armpit or not, I had to get out of there. I pushed my palms down on the chair as hard as I could and tried to get my whole body up at the same time.

"Not so fast!" Viv's mom stretched out the bandage. "We need to wrap your ankle, at least until you can go get it checked out. Otherwise the injury could become more serious. I think it's just a sprain, but we don't want it to get worse. Man, oh man," she muttered as she took the bottom half of my leg in her arms. "I've never seen so many injuries in thirty years!"

Oh, great. First it was twenty years and now it was thirty. At least she probably wasn't forty years old yet, so she couldn't make the number that much higher.

"Does anything else hurt?" she asked, handing me the ice pack for my foot.

"My, um, this area." I pointed to my armpit. I wasn't going to say "armpit" in front of Viv's mom. The day had already been embarrassing enough.

"Can you raise your arm?" she asked, and I did. "It'll be fine," she said, helping me to put my arm down by my side. "I think you just pulled a muscle. Put some ice on it when you get home and then you should be good to go. I'd take it easy on the ankle, though. You might want to stay off it for a week or so. No biking, no swimming, nothing."

"And no sitting on stationary bikes," Viv added.

"And no sitting on lounge chairs," said Kaya.

"And no sudden standing." Rafael laughed.

If Mom were here (and acting normal), she'd tell me to laugh everything off, to make fun of myself with them because they were only kidding around, and all the injury business *was* sorta funny and no one was purposely trying to make me feel like the pool fungus collecting on the bottom of my flip-flops. Well, no one except for Viv, maybe.

But Normal Mom wasn't here, and even though I knew this stuff, I couldn't make myself believe it or do it or feel it, and I didn't want to, either.

When I felt the pulsing pain of my ankle again, I knew for sure: I was done. Done with the triathlon, done with my so-called friends, done with trying to compete with Viv and her tan mom and her fancy team T-shirts. Done with my mom, too.

Done. Just done.

24
WORK

"SO, HOW ARE YOU?"

I looked up at the ceiling and tried not to roll my eyes. This question Dr. Llama asked every Saturday was starting to get annoying.

"Fine," I said. "How are you?"

As usual, he didn't answer. He just did the same old sitting and staring thing he always did, which was also starting to get annoying. But I could play that game, too.

"You seem upset," he said, after what felt like a century of silence.

"You think?" I glanced at my crutches and sighed. "I just don't want to be here right now. I have a lot of homework to do."

It was true. After Viv's mom had practically carried me home from swim practice (so embarrassing), Mom took me to the doctor, where my ankle had been wrapped tighter and fancier and I'd been told to use crutches for about a week to make sure it healed. Teachers had let me leave classes a little early to get to my next one, but that meant I missed a few minutes of each class, which was usually get-a-head-start-on-your-assignments time, which meant I ended up with more work than everyone else, which meant this weekend was going to stink even more than it already would have. And since Dr. Peterson's office was closed over the weekend, I couldn't get rid of my crutches till Monday even though I technically should have been free today. She didn't want me to stop using them till she could check on me in person.

My armpit was better now (which was lucky, because the crutches would have probably made it worse if it still hurt), but my ankle sure wasn't better after a week, and neither were the monstrous purple bruises all over my legs. BFF Britta had joked the other night that I looked like a grape monster. She wanted to paint my nails purple to match, but I didn't let her. The last thing I needed were ten little reminders of everything that had gone wrong.

"I understand," Dr. Llama said. "But you are here, so let's make the most of it. How are your bubbles?"

"Depressing," I said. I thought about his story from

last time about the queen. If I were her, and war was upon me, my castle would've been totally destroyed by now. The bubbles weren't dangerous like an actual war, but it felt like they were kicking my butt. It felt like everything was.

"There are so many sad ones," I told him. "And they make me sad." *And the happy ones make me mad,* I almost added, thinking of Kaya's news about her and Rafael. Was this how liking someone worked? You act weird, feel weird, and then eventually find out they don't like you back, or worse, like your friend instead? No wonder Mom was always so bummed about guys. Why was it so hard to find one who liked you back and then didn't ditch you for a new job or someone with hairless legs?

"You know, Sophie," Dr. Llama said, "you really care a lot about people. You're sensitive. You notice what truly goes on in people's heads, even if they don't express it on the outside."

"Well, yeah," I said. "Because of the bubbles, remember?"

He sat back in his chair. "Have you ever talked to your mom about how you feel? Or any other adults who you trust?"

I hardly heard the question; instead of listening, I stared at the teeny silver trash can in the corner of the room. There was nothing really special about it, but I couldn't look away. I'd been doing that a lot the past few days—staring. Mom did it all the time since she and Pratik broke up. She never really looked at anything in particular. She'd look at garbage cans, doors, cups of cocoa, random things. And she'd stare and stare and stare. And I never got why. I still didn't, really, but I knew that it felt like something I needed to do. The trash can didn't even look like a trash can anymore. It just looked like a big silvery blob.

That might have been because I was crying, I realized. When had I started crying?

Dr. Llama handed me a tissue. "It's okay," he said. "It's always okay to cry. Let it out." And so I did. I cried and cried until there were no more tears left in my whole entire body. I cried until Dr. Llama looked at his watch and said, "Our session is over. Great work today," and then I giggled through my tears because since when was crying considered work? But maybe it was, because when I met Mom in the waiting room I felt absolutely exhausted.

• • •

"Yoo-hoo, you there?"

I didn't answer Mom; I just nodded and kept looking

out the bus window. It was weird how crying took so much out of you. I felt totally empty, like I'd cried out not only every tear in the universe but also all my insides. If the seats on the bus were just a teeny bit comfier, I could have curled up and slept all the way home.

Mom wrapped an arm around my shoulders and gazed out the window with me.

"Hey!" she shouted out of nowhere. "We're almost at Little J's. Wanna stop?"

We hadn't been to Little J's in forever. It was an awesome ice cream place. They had the typical flavors: chocolate, vanilla, etc., and the normal toppings, but also they'd have a totally crazy Flavor of the Day, something like double chocolate bacon maple pineapple crunch, and we'd always get it no matter what it was. "You never know till you try," Mom would say. Little J's was how we discovered that cheese was amazing everywhere except ice cream. It was an important thing to learn.

I noticed some bubbles forming over a few girls across the aisle.

I wish I could fly away.

They just don't understand me.

I need to pretend everything's normal.

"Nah," I whispered to Mom. The Flavor of the Day might not be any good. We might have to wait forever for the next bus. Maybe I'd trip on a chocolate sprinkle and sprain my other ankle or knock Mom over and break one of hers. There were so many things that could go wrong in any place with any person. It was easier to stay put, to close my eyes, to keep the bubbles out.

To keep everything out.

• • •

"Hi, girls!"

Ms. Wolfson was getting home at the same time we got off the bus. I gave her a little wave with one of my crutches, and Mom flashed her a teeny smile.

She gave both of us a look. "Well, aren't you two bundles of joy. What's wrong?"

I didn't say anything. Mom didn't say anything. Ms. Wolfson sighed.

"Let's play cribbage," she said.

Now Mom found her voice. "We . . . can't . . . right now." She sounded about as convincing as Benedict Arnold probably did when he was all *No, you guys are wrong, I'm not a spy.* Nobody believed him, and Ms. Wolfson definitely didn't believe us.

"That wasn't a question," she said. "But, Molly, you are excused. I'm sure you have things you need to do."

And I didn't?

I groaned as we followed her inside. Mom waved and went up to our place, leaving me with Ms. Wolfson. This was so unfair. Yeah, I liked her, but I didn't feel like hanging out right now. I bet no one ever made King Edward VI play cribbage if he didn't want to. (He became king of England and Ireland when he was nine years old, so he had a ton of stuff he had to do. But so did I!)

"I had quite a day today myself," Ms. Wolfson said as she dealt the cards. "Seems like everybody in the world is upset about something."

I had to pick two of my cards to put into the crib, the secret stash of cards you got to see at the end of the game, but it was hard to concentrate with her talking.

"The person driving behind me wouldn't stop honking for miles. Some woman yelled at me for taking the last copy of a book at the library, like she owned it or something. Which she didn't. Just one of those days, I guess." She glanced at me. "Eyes on your own cards, Sophie."

But my cards looked blurry. How could she concentrate on hers when she had all that other stuff going on? And how could I?

I took a breath and made myself look down to see what I had.

"So?" she asked. "What are you going to do?"

I wanted to say, "Nothing." I wanted to do nothing. But it felt like that wasn't really a choice. So I focused on my cards, and thought about them, and after a few minutes, I made my move.

And Ms. Wolfson made hers.

And it wasn't bad at all.

25
TRUTH

THE NEXT WEEK WAS SPRING BREAK. I DIDN'T FEEL LIKE doing much except going to play cribbage with Ms. Wolfson. Between all of Mom's Pratik stuff and my Rafael and Kaya and Viv stuff and everybody else's millions of things they were sad about, it was obviously better to keep things simple, to do as little as you could instead of doing things and wishing you hadn't. If I did that, I wouldn't end up feeling sad like everybody else.

I tried not to notice that I already did.

The good news was I was off my crutches long before school started up again. The bad news was that once it did, all Kaya, Rafael, and their new BFF Viv wanted to talk about was the triathlon, and all the millions of practices they'd had over break without me (because my ankle still hurt), and all the zillions of inside jokes they had from those practices. Every time I tried to get into the conversation, they'd start talking about their hilarious running and biking adventures. Which, spoiler alert, were actually not hilarious at all. Especially the fact that Kaya and Viv had taught Rafael to ride a real bike, and now he was a pro, and I'd missed the whole thing.

As the week went on, I started walking by them without stopping.

And maybe the only thing worse than that was the fact that no one cared.

Kaya seemed happier than ever. And why wouldn't she be? She'd crushed it on the bike and in the pool— and had a secret boyfriend, now, too, and had probably done lots of secret boyfriend/girlfriend things over break. She was acting like a whole different person. She skalloped instead of walked. She sat up straighter, talked a lot more in class, and wore her hair down instead of up in a high ponytail or topknot.

She didn't twirl it around, either. Sometimes, yeah, but really not often at all.

It should've made me really, really happy. Every time I saw a bubble over her head, it was a good one. *I'm having the best day. I can't believe how great everything is. My life is so cool.*

But it was weird when your best friend was happier

and better and less nervous and more adventurous and you didn't have a single thing to do with it.

At least I had a distraction. There were bubbles everywhere at school lately. (They probably would've been everywhere over break, too, but I hadn't really gone anywhere except Dr. Llama's and Ms. Wolfson's.) And while it was pretty exciting knowing everyone's secrets, it felt stressful, too. Like a lot of responsibility I didn't ask for. I bet Mr. Clements, the school librarian, wouldn't even know what to do with all that information, and he knew everything.

Sometimes I heard Ms. Wolfson's voice in my head. *Eyes on your own cards, Sophie.*

But what did you do when it felt like you were in charge of holding everyone's decks?

26
LITTLE WINS

"WANT TO GO SHOPPING?"

I didn't. I wanted to sit around and mope and feel sorry for myself. I was crankier than Napoleon must've been after the Battle of Waterloo, which he lost really bad. So no, Mom, I did not want to go shopping one bit.

But then I looked up from my magazine and really noticed her. There wasn't a bubble to give me any more detailed information, but she looked *better*. She'd straightened her hair and made a braid crown across the top. She was wearing a cute outfit and had a teeny bit of makeup on. Her face sparkled more than it had in ages.

"Well?" She put her hands on her hips and made a puppy-dog-begging face. I knew I owed her big-time, but I still didn't want to.

"Call Britta."

"I want to go with you. What's wrong? I never thought I'd have to beg you to shop, especially on a Sunday after you've gotten your thirteen hours of sleep. Bubbles got you down?"

I sighed in a pretend-mad way and ignored the bubble question. "I actually prefer fifteen hours of sleep."

"Just one store," she promised. "Cross my heart. I want to pick up a new workout outfit at ZOOM. If you're going to sit and be mopey, you can do that while being surrounded by pretty things we can't afford."

"You want to go to ZOOM?" I raised my eyebrows. It cost like eighty dollars for a headband at ZOOM. And a hundred bucks per glove, I remembered, thinking of Rafael.

"Yes," Mom said firmly. "It's Buy Yourself a Present Day. All the Adventurous Girls do it."

Then why were we going to do it?

I peeled my legs off the couch and glanced at Mom again. Her braid crown was super cute and she did seem different, but I didn't know if I really bought it. Sometimes there were false alarms—she'd act all perky and fun and like herself, usually when she went somewhere with Britta, but then she'd be all sniffly again before the night was over. I thought back to Weird Whimper

Night and shuddered to myself. I couldn't deal with that again. Just thinking about her making noises like that made *me* want to make noises like that, too.

But if I didn't go to ZOOM with her, would she start doing that sooner?

"Okay," I finally agreed. "But I'm finding a place to sit and I'm staying there the whole time."

"Deal."

. . .

True to her word, Mom helped me find the couch at ZOOM by the dressing rooms and held on to my arm until I got my ankle all elevated and comfortable. I wished couches came with seat belts. It was a nice couch, but it was also the kind of couch I could totally see myself rolling right off, probably at the same moment that Viv or her mom or their spinning friends randomly appeared.

I looked around nervously. I hadn't thought about the spinning people until now, but this totally seemed like the kind of place where they'd hang out when they weren't at the gym. After all, those fancy outfits and shoes had to come from somewhere, and this was exactly the type of place where they'd get them.

"Do you like this?" In only ten minutes, Mom had

run back and forth about twelve million times with a whole bunch of different shorts-and-T-shirt combinations.

"Yup," I said for the millionth time. The truth was, they all kinda looked the same to me, but I definitely wasn't going to tell that to her.

She looked at herself in the giant mirror.

"I don't know. It's a little bunchy. Excuse me," she called to a passing salesgirl who didn't look that much older than me. "Do you have this pink tank in a smaller size?"

The salesgirl smacked her gum super loud and rolled her eyes. "Um, no. You're wearing an extra small. That's as small as they go." She made a huffy kind of laugh sound and walked away.

"Well. That was rude," Mom said.

I could tell she was trying not to be sad, but she was totally sad. Her whole body wilted and her eyes got that twitchy I'm-about-to-cry look in them that I knew so well. The scary thing about it was that it didn't just happen when she was thinking about Pratik. It could happen over anything these past few months, even things that seemed not that important, like a snotty salesgirl.

I knew this was a bad idea. I should never have agreed to come. I should have stayed on the couch at home and forced Mom to stay there with me.

A bubble formed over Mom's head right then.

I'm doing the best I can. Why is everybody out to get me? Why can't one thing go right?

Something weird came over me then, the strongest, most serious I-need-to-do-something-and-I-need-to-do-it-now feeling ever. It bubbled up and fizzled over faster than the massive eruption of Mount Vesuvius thousands of years ago. Mom was really trying, I could tell. This wasn't a false alarm. She wanted to go out and do something and she wanted to have fun and she was doing everything she could not to cry. Yeah, maybe it would have been better to stay home, but we were here, this store and this salesgirl and the rudeness were upon us, and it wasn't okay.

Forgetting all about my ankle, I leaped off the couch and chased the girl out of the dressing rooms and all the way to the other end of the store. My feet got a little tangled up in each other as I sprinted, and they seemed to really want to crash into the tall plastic tree over by the hats. I stretched my arm as far as it would go and tapped the salesgirl on the shoulder. Then I fell into the fake tree.

"Excuse you," I said, in the most serious voice you can use when you're covered in fake dirt.

She turned around and rolled her eyes again. "Yeah?"

I stood up and brushed myself off. This girl probably thought I was the biggest weirdo ever, but right now it almost didn't matter.

"You were rude to my mom," I said. "I know maybe it's annoying to you that she wanted a smaller size, but she's going through a hard time, and it's kind of a big deal that she even wanted to come here today. So . . ." My voice trailed off. I didn't know what else to say. But something had to be said, and now it had been.

"Oh." The girl shifted back and forth on her fancy lime-green sneakers. I wondered if they were for running or spinning or what. Maybe they were special for wandering around giant stores. I was sure Viv had a pair of those, too. "I'm sorry," she told me. "I didn't know."

"Well, now you do," I said, noticing the bubble forming over her head.

Your mom isn't the only sad one.

"And, uh, I'm sorry, too," I said. "Just, for, like, anything in your life that's going on that's hard."

Before I knew what was happening, the girl's arms were around me. She was hugging me. The not-so-snotty salesgirl was full-on hugging me.

"Thank you," she said when she pulled back. There were tears in her eyes. "Everyone thinks I'm fine since it's been so long since it happened." She stared at the fake tree plant the way Mom stared at cocoa. "My dog, Teddy Roosevelt, died," she explained. "I've had him almost my entire life."

I raised my eyebrows. "Teddy Roosevelt?"

Her face turned red. "Yeah. I'm really into history."

"So am I."

"Really? Awesome!"

Who knew? Not only was the snotty salesgirl not so snotty, we also had something in common.

"Do you want another hug?" I held out my arms, and she practically fell into them.

When she pulled away, she smiled at me. "Tell your mom I can order an extra-extra small from our Old Orchard location. It should be here within the week."

"Thanks."

. . .

"Where'd you run off to? And should I even ask about the dirt?" Mom was still in the dressing room area, but she wasn't trying anything on. She was sitting on the wobbly couch I somehow hadn't fallen off or tripped over. That reminded me—my ankle. I reached down and rubbed it. It actually felt okay. Normal. Better than normal.

"I just wanted to ask her about that shirt again," I said. "It was super cute on you. She said they can order a smaller one and you can get it this week. Oh, and I fell into a tree, but I'm okay. It wasn't a real tree."

Mom's eyes lit up.

"Why are you so excited that I fell into a tree?"

She laughed. "Sorry. I'm just happy about the shirt. It's nice to get a win, you know? Even if it's a little one."

"An extra-extra small one," I agreed, thinking about the shirt. I smiled. "Definitely counts."

I knew exactly what she meant. For the first time in a while, I had done something using all my energy and all my heart—and it felt great. It wasn't that hard, either. I just had to act like I cared. And it wasn't even an act—I really did care. Of course, caring didn't bring back Teddy Roosevelt or anything. But it brought back the salesgirl's smile. And that was pretty cool.

Mom ended up leaving with one of the eighty-dollar headbands (there was one on clearance for fifteen) and I got a really cute purple water bottle with sparkles on the sides. As we were checking out at the register, I noticed a big sign advertising the triathlon. I shouldn't have been surprised to see it; after all, ZOOM Athletics was a sponsor, and they were offering that massive prize for the winners. But there it was, staring me right in the eyes.

Mom noticed it, too.

"Is that the race you and your friends are doing?" She handed her credit card over to No-Longer-Snotty Salesgirl, and I looked at her. She knew? She'd actually heard me when I told her I was going to practices, even when she was staring off into space?

"There's an adult race, too," she mumbled, more to herself than anyone else. Where was Mom going with this? She hadn't done a race in forever. She hadn't looked at the stuff in her box in forever. She hadn't done anything in forever. She couldn't seriously be thinking . . .

"Can I sign up for this?" Mom asked.

No-Longer-Snotty Salesgirl laughed. "You're in luck," she said. "Today's April first, the last day to register!"

Mom looked at me and grinned. "You mind if I do the adult triathlon? I doubt I'll be any good, but it'd be fun to try."

I didn't know what to say. That was exactly what I wanted, sorta. Mom wanted to do something again! And I hadn't even had to run the race to convince her. Just by trying my risk, my risk had paid off.

But maybe it wasn't over yet. If Mom was after little wins—and felt this good when she got one—what would it be like if she got a Big Win? What would it be like if I got one with her? Together?

And what would happen if we didn't?

Maybe it was even riskier than it was before.

"You're still in, right?" Mom stuck her credit card back in her wallet, filled out the form, and handed it to the salesgirl. Even with nerves rattling around inside me like cool historical coins, I made myself nod.

Mom grabbed her bag, smiled at No-Longer-Snotty, and hugged me harder than she had in a long time.

"I'm so excited to do this together," she whispered into my hair.

And for the first time in forever, with Mom's arm linked through mine as we walked to the bus stop, even though it was going to be super tough for me to win the race—or even to just do the race—for a minute it felt like anything was possible.

27

YOU CAN RUN BUT
YOU CAN'T HIDE

GOING TO WPA WITH MOM AFTER SCHOOL WAS TOTALLY different than going with my friends. I wasn't worried about anything. I was curious about what kind of injury I'd get next, but not stressed. Plus I had my snazzy ZOOM water bottle with me, so even if I broke my face or something, I'd be hydrating in style.

Mom seemed pretty nervous, though. She was all decked out in her I-mean-business ZOOM headband and hot-pink tank (the extra-extra small came just in time), but she kept looking around like some terrifying Gym Monster of Doom was going to jump out and attack her at any second.

"What are you doing?" I asked. "Some kind of weird triathlon stretch?" I was fairly sure that you didn't run with your head, but Mom probably knew a bunch of tricks that I didn't. We turned down a long hallway I'd never seen before. WPA was humongous. I thought we'd seen it all, but there was still more to discover around every corner.

"It's nothing," Mom said, finally looking straight ahead at the room we were going into, where a giant oval-shaped track stretched from one end to the other. If I was going to fall here, it'd be because of my own two feet and nothing else. Just how I liked it.

Mom still looked nervous. Her face was splotchy red and a little green, like a Christmas tree we should've taken down a long time ago.

"Are you going to throw up?" I didn't really see anywhere for her to do that here.

"No. It's just . . ." Mom looked around some more. "This is Pratik's gym, too. We used to come here together."

Ohhhh. Now everything made sense. Why she had taken longer getting ready for this than I took getting ready for school on picture day. Why her head wouldn't stop spinning around. Why she was more jumpy than the people at NASA probably were before they sent the first astronauts to the moon in 1969.

"I don't see him anywhere, do you?" Mom asked. I glanced around. This was totally the worst floor for us to be hanging out on. There were doors everywhere, and people poured in and out from almost every direction. Had there always been so many doors? If I ever opened my own gym, my own anything, it would have one door and one door only, and a security person standing there who would alert everyone inside if somebody appeared who they didn't want to see.

"Don't see him," I told her, but I knew it wasn't going to help. Just because I didn't see him right this second didn't mean he wasn't going to show up at all.

"I don't want him to think that I'm following him around or something."

Maybe this was why I used Mom's gym membership way more than she ever did.

"Mom, he doesn't own the place."

I crossed my fingers behind my back. I didn't actually know what Pratik did in his vice president job. For all I knew, maybe he *did* own the place, and wanted to go overseas to build more fancy gyms with way too many doors.

Mom wandered over to the track's starting line. I gulped and stared down at my sneakers. I had known going into this that running was going to be my worst thing, but now that I'd seen how bad I was at swimming and biking . . . well, it couldn't get much worse than that, could it?

I had a sinking feeling that maybe it could.

But today was different. I had Mom with me. When she used to do triathlons, we crossed the finish lines together. I'd wait there with BFF Britta or Pratik or whatever guy Mom was going out with at the time, and when I saw her neon-purple tank top coming at me, I'd go out into the street, grab her hand, and we'd make a mad dash for the end.

My feet always got so tangled up in each other when I tried to run by myself, but holding on to Mom steadied me, somehow. When she dragged me toward the finish line, I always made it there. We did it together, but I only really did it because of her.

I knew I'd have to run my race without her, but maybe some of her skill would rub off on me during practice.

Mom stretched her arms to her sides and followed their motion slowly with her head. She was pretty sneaky, but not sneaky enough to fool me.

"You should have to do another lap every time you look at the doors," I said.

She laughed. "I'm busted, huh?"

"Very busted."

"There are just so many guys around here who look like him."

I made a serious face. "Mom, Wolfson women are not doormats."

"What?"

I laughed to myself. I hadn't thought about it in a while, and it was a really weird thing to say out loud. But it just seemed like something Mom needed to hear.

"Ms. Wolfson said it to me once. I think it just means, like, don't let anyone else be the boss of you and put gross stuff from their shoes on you. Like if something bugs you, don't just sit there and take it."

"Oh." Mom smiled. "Okay. Thanks, Soph. You're right. I don't even know why it's bugging me—he's probably traveling for his job. And even if he is here, I shouldn't hide. I should . . ."—she eyed the track—"run." She said it again. "I should run."

"Me too."

"Are you ready?"

"Are you?"

Mom and I looked at each other. Were we ready? No. Not at all, probably never would be, and we both knew it. But we were here, and we weren't doormats, and we were going to do a triathlon.

"Ready," we said together, and, with a quick nod and glance at each other, we were off.

28
ERUPTION

MOM LOOKED ALMOST AS CLUELESS AS I FELT GOING down the track. She kept glancing at her feet like she'd never seen them before in her life and had no idea what she was supposed to do with them.

My feet, on the other hand, were actually behaving for once in their lives. It was super confusing. I thought I would have gone *splat* on the ground in two seconds flat. I thought I'd be a human pancake, stomped on and smashed by all the real runners' feet before I even realized how pancake-y I was.

But I wasn't a pancake.

I was hungry for them, for sure, with bananas and chocolate chips, but I hadn't turned into one. Yet.

It was a very nice surprise.

I tried to stay with Mom, but she was going way too

slow. She waved me forward with her hand and told me to go ahead. So I did. I ran. Past a whole bunch of other people. Around the track once and twice and a third time. Again and again and again and again. I thought of Kaya and Rafael and Viv and injuries and being terrible at things and being left out and seeing bubbles and therapists and stress and doing too much and not doing enough and I imagined myself putting all of it behind me in a humongous box and I imagined everything staying put in that box as I sprinted ahead and around and away. I know you're not supposed to run away from your problems, but I wasn't doing that. I was just putting them down for a second. And it felt like nothing I'd ever felt before.

I caught up to Mom after I'd made another lap around her. She was huffing and puffing like crazy.

"I . . . am . . . so . . . out . . . of . . . shape," she said, with a massive breath between each word. She slowed down more until she totally stopped. "Keep going, Soph," Mom told me. "You're doing amazing. And I'm fine. Really."

She was right. I *was* doing amazing. Running was amazing.

But she wasn't fine.

There was a bubble over her head almost immediately.

I hate this. I'm never going to make it around. Why am I even trying?

I looked at Mom. Even in her awesome new tank top from ZOOM, this was Stare at Stuff Mom running around this track, not the real Molly Mulvaney.

I was about to take off again—what else could I do?—when I got an idea.

"Mom, remember when we used to play that game where we pretended that I was an erupting volcano and you were the townspeople?" I giggled just thinking about it. We always wanted to go see a real volcano, but they were too far away and it cost too much money to go to any of them. So instead we'd settle for me shouting *"Eruption!"* at the top of my lungs and chasing Mom all over our apartment, then collapsing in a fit of giggles and hugs like three hours later.

I watched her face break into a smile. She remembered!

"Well . . ." I said, getting ready. *"Eruption!"*

I charged at Mom with every shred of energy I had left. She shuffled forward, and soon her shuffle turned into a jog, and her jog turned into a full-on sprint.

"Not so fast, townspeople!" I hollered, pushing myself harder. I was running faster than I ever had in my life. It was like my legs had a mind of their own, plus a whole bunch of strength and power I never knew existed. Where had these legs been hiding during gym class all this time? And all the other times when I tried to run?

We ran and ran and ran and somehow never ran out of energy. I don't know about Mom, but I forgot about all the other people in the gym, and all the other people everywhere, too. I forgot about bubbles and therapists and Kaya and Rafael and Viv and sadness and stress and doing too much and not enough and the possibility of serious injury. I even forgot where I was for a minute, which was a very bad move, because, as I was thinking about absolutely nothing, I crashed right into Mom.

Who had stopped because she had crashed right into Pratik.

· · ·

"Hey, you two," he said, like it was no big deal that Mom had knocked him flat on the ground. He jumped up and brushed himself off. "Interesting way to start my workout. How are you?"

No. No. No no no no no.

I grabbed on to Mom's hand and pulled her up. She had to be totally embarrassed, but it was kinda funny in a weird way. After everything Mom had done to make sure we didn't see him at home, there he was, at the gym, the second we finally forgot about him. He looked different since I'd seen him last. Shorter hair. Fancier shoes. But he was definitely still Pratik.

"I'm good," Mom said in a way-too-happy kind of voice.

"I'm good," I echoed.

"I . . . um." It was like Mom had forgotten how to talk all of a sudden. "Sorry I knocked you down. Are you okay?"

"Yeah, fine."

I could practically see Mom's heart tumbling out of her chest. If we couldn't do it, maybe Mom's heart could win the triathlon. That thing was speedy.

My heart was beating a little fast, too, and my eyes couldn't stop staring at Pratik. There was something else different about him. It was the way he looked at us, like we could be any of the moms and daughters at the gym. Like we were strangers who'd just met and were having some dumb little gym conversation. But we weren't! We were *us*! How could you have so many fun times with someone and then just act like everything was whatever, like none of it had even happened?

And why were we still so bummed over someone who was clearly not bummed at all over us?

A bubble formed over Pratik's head, and I grabbed

on to Mom's arm almost automatically, bracing myself. Whatever it was going to say, I had a feeling it was going to be really important.

I wonder if there's anything good on TV later.

TV?

Seriously?

I knew it, though. TV didn't seem super important, but that's what made it important. He was thinking about TV. Not about us. Not about how we might be feeling. Not about how he was feeling. Just . . . TV. And that was it.

Mom gave me a look like "What's up with the death grip?" and I gave her one back like "We need to talk, big-time," and she nodded.

Holy. Chocolate-iest. Pancakes. In. The. Universe.

Mom understood what my face was telling her.

That Colossus of Rhodes thing that crumbled all those years ago? It never got rebuilt, but there's a plan to do it soon. Maybe everything can get rebuilt if you give people enough time to figure out the right way to do it.

"Okay. I gotta run," Mom told Pratik. She chuckled awkwardly. "I gotta run," she repeated, eyeing the track. "Like I actually gotta run."

Pratik laughed. "All right," he said. "Good to see you. You too, Sophie."

He walked away in the direction of the stairs. Mom

turned her attention back to the track, but I watched him walk away and wondered where he was going. Swimming? Spinning? Maybe Pratik didn't know where he was going either, I realized. But he kept moving, just like we did, even though we were tired. Maybe sometimes that's all you can do.

29

THE STUFF YOU KNOW

"OKAY, WHAT'D YOU SEE IN THE BUBBLE? SPILL IT."

I fiddled with the string on my pajama bottoms. We were home now, safely on the couch, icing all our hurting parts and stretching out our sleepy, sleepy legs, which were probably going to be super sore tomorrow. I smiled to myself, thinking about it. It was cool that my legs were going to hurt because I had actually used them for something besides falling over. I had used them for actual exercise, for *running*, of all things! I couldn't wait to get to school tomorrow so I could tell my gym teacher.

I took a deep breath. Mom deserved to know this stuff. I didn't know if it would make her happy or sad or excited or what, but it was too much to keep in my brain, and she was asking, and there wasn't anyone else

I could tell who would truly get it like she would. But there was something I had to ask first.

"Do you only want to know because it's about Pratik?"

Mom frowned. "I want to know because you're my daughter and I care about you."

"Then why haven't you really asked about any other bubbles?"

She took a deep breath. "I think I owe you an apology. I really haven't been there for you lately. It's not just Pratik . . . it's a lot of things. But none of it's an excuse."

"You're allowed to be sad," I told her. "You should be mad at me, too. Super mad. Since I'm the reason you guys broke up."

"What?"

"Because I was like, oh, I'm gonna be this cool spy person, and then I went and squealed about his new job and then you got in a fight and he dumped you, remember?"

Mom's eyes got enormous. "Sophie, no. No!"

I raised my eyebrows. No? As in . . . no?

"Yeah, we argued that day, but things were tough before that. You never noticed how we had started to hardly speak to each other when we were together?"

I thought about it. That day, Pratik had been on the couch, doing a crossword puzzle. Mom had been in the kitchen making pancakes. It *looked* normal, but they were in different rooms, doing different things, not saying much . . . on purpose?

"He just stopped telling me things over time. I had no idea he got a new job, or even that he wanted one. I want to be with someone who tells me things—even the things that are hard to say."

"Then why did you go out for so long? And why did *he* dump *you*?"

Mom shrugged. "I loved the guy. Sometimes you know everything in the world, but if the way you feel doesn't match up, the stuff you know ends up not mattering at all." She paused. "He really did us a favor, Soph, even though it's been hard to adjust."

I shuddered. It sounded like love did super weird things to people. Being in like was more than enough for me, especially being in like with someone who was going out with somebody else.

I fiddled with my pajama strings some more. "Do you still want to know what his bubble said?" I asked.

Mom played with a few pieces of my hair. "You know, I don't think I do," she said. "Unless you want to tell me."

"I don't think it really matters," I said. "Do you?"

"I think the person whose thoughts I want to know the most is the person sitting next to me. You can tell me anything, Soph, always. The good, the bad . . ."

"The bubbly?" I interrupted, and she laughed. We both did.

Mom pulled the blanket up so we each had just enough. Her words echoed in my mind. *The stuff you know ends up not mattering at all.* I knew what I knew about Kaya and Rafael, but I knew what I felt, too.

And that's when I knew what I had to do.

30

AN UPDATE

IN SCHOOL THE NEXT DAY, MR. ALVARADO ASKED FOR AN update on our projects.

"Mine's going really well." Obviously Viv was the first to chime in. Kaya shot her a big smile.

Viv wasn't kidding. In case I needed her to rub it in any more, practically every time I'd looked at her all morning there had been something project-related floating above her head in a bubble.

I have them right where I want them.

Now I just have to work on one more thing.

This is the greatest project ever.

I am awesome!

I still didn't know what I was going to do about her, or if I even could do something about her. But I could do something about Kaya and Rafael.

I scurried after Kaya in the hall and grabbed her by the arm. I had to talk to her before we met up with Rafael or the whole thing would be wrecked. "I saw a major bubble. Like a crazy one. And a serious one. A crazy, serious, major bubble." Okay, I had to chill. I was going to be out of breath by the time I got to my actual news.

"Oh yeah?" Kaya's eyes grew wide and I felt a teeny tiny twisty twinge of guilt. I didn't do bad things like this, especially not to one of my best friends. But she had started it when she decided to go out with Rafael and they told Viv instead of me.

"Yeah. At the end of the day yesterday. Above Rafael's head . . ."

As usual, I was awful at lying, but Kaya, ever the trusting one, nodded like she couldn't wait to hear what I would say next.

There was a major garlic-knotty feeling in my stomach, but I kept going.

"It said that he likes Viv."

Kaya's face scrunched up really tight, like she was getting ready to cry. She reached for her head but flung her hands down at the last second. Like a little voice in her brain was like, *No, Kaya. Control yourself.* Like the little voice in my brain should have done but didn't, because it was too busy being like, *Cause problems!*

195

It was a really good thing Kaya couldn't see bubbles above my head. I bet the letters would all have been bold and capitalized. ***I'M LYING.***

But Kaya didn't ask any questions, and I felt bad and good at the same time because I wanted to do this but I didn't totally want to do this, and maybe this was actually a really awful thing to do that I should have never, ever done.

I was in a tug-of-war with myself, all of a sudden, the part that wanted to come clean and the other part that wanted to see how this would go. Both of them were pulling, pulling, pulling, and if there had been a real rope involved, it would have snapped in two, leaving little ropy thread thingies all over the place.

Kaya tucked her head down and stared at the floor. She didn't say a thing. It was as quiet as the Cold War. (Which was called that because people fought with words instead of with weapons.)

"Are you okay?" I asked. "I mean, there's not any major reason this would bother you, is there?"

She didn't make eye contact with me but kept shuffling along by my side.

"Kaya? Answer please?"

There was a ton of hallway noise surrounding us, but I couldn't hear it. The whole world seemed silent to me just because Kaya was.

We rounded a corner and got to our spot. Finally, Kaya looked me right in the eye and opened her mouth . . .

Just as Rafael flew down the stairs, practically trampled an entire clump of people, and yelled at the top of his lungs, "We can't do the triathlon!"

"What?" I said.

"What?" Kaya repeated.

"What?" said Viv, who'd just run up.

"My cousin Harmony forwarded me her confirmation e-mail from the race people and asked if I was still doing it or if I'd chickened out. But, guys, I didn't *get* a confirmation e-mail. Did you?"

We all shook our heads, and my stomach started doing flip-flops. Why did this kinda sound like something that might be my fault? Was there something I was supposed to do? Something about confirmations or registrations or . . .

Holy pancakes. Registrations.

"I called ZOOM to check and they said they didn't have any of our registration forms, and they won't accept any late ones," Rafael said. "We can't sign up the day of the race, either." My stomach flipped harder and faster. I could picture the registration forms. They were buried at the bottom of my backpack with old snacks and papers and who knew what else.

I heard my own voice in my head, agreeing to turn in

the forms. I remembered them all nodding and smiling and saying thanks. I remembered Viv dropping hers in my hand. I remembered putting it in my backpack with the others and then completely forgetting and not doing anything with any of them, even when I was at ZOOM on the day of the deadline with Mom.

We stood there silently. It was my fault. It was totally my fault. One of my biggest fears had come true. I'd messed up the triathlon, just like I'd thought I would.

"I'm sorry," I whispered. "I forgot to turn in the forms."

No one said anything. Rafael and Kaya looked at each other, and Viv glared at me. It wasn't even her project, but she looked the angriest out of everyone.

"You guys are going to have to figure out another risk," she said. "Otherwise you'll probably fail social studies."

"Yeah, for real." Rafael crossed his arms and looked at the ground.

"Mmm-hmm." Kaya twirled a chunk of hair around her finger.

I didn't want to admit it, but Viv Carlson was right. This was an assignment. A good grade would be cool, but it was even more important not to let down Mr. Alvarado. He was one of everybody's favorite teachers, and he'd be so disappointed if we didn't do the race. I thought of how excited he was, of how he had pulled Kaya, Viv, and me aside yesterday after class and told us how people in all his classes were making plans to come watch.

Well, all they'd be watching was a bunch of depressed people sitting on the sidelines. Lucky them. Plus, there was Mom. I needed to win to give her a chance to get on TV. And she'd actually been really excited to do the race together. Would she still do it if she knew she'd be totally on her own?

I couldn't take the chance.

I looked at Kaya and Rafael. Their eyes finally met mine, and I could tell they were trying not to come out and be all OMG-we-hate-you-Sophie, but I had definitely caused a big problem—and everybody knew it.

Only instead of feeling bad about it forever the way I had about Mom's breakup (which wasn't even my fault), I was going to fix it.

Starting in 1848, a ton of people went to California because they heard there was gold there and they wanted it. Some of the people gave up right away. Others looked for a while and then gave up. But some stayed and kept looking until they found it.

Maybe I could be one of those people.

The thing with gold was that it usually didn't just

pop up with a giant sign that said HEY, I'M GOLD. You had to look under stuff. Around stuff. Sort through a bunch of rocks that kinda looked like gold but weren't.

"I have an idea," I told everyone.

Then I turned away and raced toward the school library, stumbling over my feet the entire way. There had to be gold hiding in this situation somewhere, and I needed to be the one to find it.

If I did, it would be the coolest thing in history.

31
THE NEW PROJECT

I COULDN'T STAY IN THE LIBRARY FOR TOO LONG SINCE I had other classes to go to, but I was able to go back at lunch and collect a ton of info. With our librarian's help, I researched some triathlon-y stuff online and looked through a bunch of helpful books, and before long, I had an actual semi-realistic idea for a new project.

Once I had figured out some details after school, my semi-realistic idea moved into could-totally-happen territory. And after I'd made some phone calls and sent some texts, it was officially going to be a thing.

At least, it was going to be a thing until the responses started trickling in.

Sry, I want 2 do something else. Thinking of risky things 2 do 2 make $$$ 4 gloves. GLOVES RULE

I rolled my eyes. Okay, Rafael.

Cool idea but gonna help Raf w/his thing

My face felt warm. I knew neither Rafael nor Kaya were super happy with me, but I was trying to help! I'd found the gold, but now nobody wanted it.

At least BFF Britta agreed that my idea was awesome. She even told Mom that she should help out, but Mom just sighed and was all, "We'll see," and went back to whatever magazine she was reading.

And when I asked, "You're still doing ZOOM's adult triathlon, right? Even though I can't do the kid one?" Mom didn't answer at all.

I sat on my bed and buried my head in my hands. So no one was interested in my idea. Fine. But the fact was, I had to do a risk project or probably fail sixth grade. And whatever Rafael and Kaya were planning now, it didn't seem like I was exactly invited.

So. Even if I did it all by myself, I was going to do it.

I, Sophie Elizabeth Mulvaney, was going to do a triathlon.

32
TRI TIME

"ARE YOU TOTALLY SURE YOU DON'T WANT TO DO IT? YOU would be so awesome. Come on. Please?"

But Mom shook her head and slipped her fuzzy black jacket on over her pink tank. "I'm just going to watch you, and that's it."

The real triathlons had come and gone, and Mom had stayed on the couch with her magazines. The winners went on TV, and Mom didn't watch. Even though Mom was talking to me more now, she was still sad. So this was more than my risk project; this was my last real chance to turn her back into Mom Who Does More Than Stare at Stuff.

"Why aren't you asking if I want to try it?" BFF Britta smirked and zipped up her purple fleece, and we all giggled. Her idea of a triathlon was watching three movies in a row.

"You can," I said. "Really. Everyone who tries gets a prize." That was the official slogan of my new and improved triathlon. I had stayed up late last night making fancy certificates with markers and paint and a ton of glitter glue. The droopy eyelids and weirdly sore cheeks were totally worth it, because they looked amazing. I was probably going to be the only one there besides Mom, Britta, and Mr. Alvarado, but I wanted to be ready for anything.

"Who are you, Dr. Seuss?" Now Britta was giggling harder. "Run the race, yes you can! Go the miles, get a tan!"

"Not such great tanning weather today." Mom peeked out the window. Of course the day had to go and be all dreary and gloomy—the sky was covered with clouds. Not so great for doing a triathlon, even a mini one. Or for going outside at all. At least the temperature wasn't terrible. We all just needed light jackets, nothing more, but I shivered as I thought about the swimming. That was going to be soooo cold. I could have been all cozy in Dr. Llama's office, but I was skipping therapy to do something I knew was going to be hard. Why was I torturing myself like this?

I already knew the answer to that, though. I was

doing this for Kaya and Rafael. If they weren't going to swim and bike, I'd do it in their honor. I was doing it for Mom. Even for Viv Carlson. For all the people with bubbles, especially people with sad ones. And maybe I was doing it a little for me, too.

I needed to do it. Even if every bone in my body was scared, achy, and about to totally freeze.

"Ready?" Britta squeezed my shoulders. "It's cool that you're doing this, Mini Mulvaney."

"You're an Adventurous Girl," Mom said. I knew it was a compliment—I *was* an Adventurous Girl again, now—but something about it made me sad. Yeah, she was saying I was adventurous, but it also sort of seemed like she was saying she wasn't.

Which was the truth. But still.

Now was no time for sadness, though.

I had a race to get to.

. . .

Bridgemont Beach was practically deserted. An old couple walked a dog along the path, but they were the only people I could see for miles. I gulped. Where was everybody? I snuck a glance at my phone—7:02. Kaya and Rafael probably wouldn't show up, but what was Mr. Alvarado's excuse? He was a teacher; he was used to getting up early. He probably even did it on Saturdays when he didn't have to.

"You knew this was a possibility. This was pretty short notice, and you only told what, a few people? Your friends and your teacher?" Mom put her hand on my shoulder. Britta shivered and snuggled up next to her.

I nodded. I had only told a few people, but they were important people.

"At least you can still do it," I said to Mom, but she just shook her head.

The three of us walked to the water in silence. The wind picked up, because obviously being regular-gross out wasn't enough. Mom's hair flopped around all over the place.

A bubble came up above her head. *I wish I were strong enough.*

I took a big gulp of cold air and unzipped my hoodie. Fine. Everyone else could be a wimp. Even if Mom didn't do the race, she'd see it. I'd do it for her, for everybody, even if that meant I did it totally alone. Because I *was* strong enough.

Shivering, I slid down my sweatpants and tossed them on the ground along with my hoodie.

"Well, ready, set, go," I said to myself, walking to the water. This was so unexciting. But whatever. I'd get my good grade. I'd have tried to make it right with everybody and really help Mom.

I had kinda hoped that planning my own triathlon would make everybody really excited, though. Like they'd be all, *Forget that dumb ZOOM Athletics triathlon! This race will be way better!* and maybe they'd feel less scared of the things that freaked them out, and everybody would show up.

I thought since there wasn't any pressure to win, it would be fun for everybody. But it'd still be risky. It *was* risky, in lots of different ways. And now, as I was seeing, it was one of those risks that didn't pay off. Because no one liked my idea and now here I was, all alone, about to freeze my butt off for no real reason at all.

I thought about the Boston Tea Party, and I wondered what had happened next, like after it ended. I knew it led to the Revolutionary War, but not the details in between. Maybe they got what they wanted. Or maybe they just did their tea thing and went on their way and nothing changed. Could that be how some stories ended? Dr. Llama had never really told me what happened with that queen and her war. Maybe the war happened, and then it ended, and that was that.

I always pictured things with happily ever afters, or at least with the hope of a sequel or something if the ending to the first one wasn't that good. But maybe some things just ended. People tried things and they didn't work and they went on their way. Sometimes sadly, like Mom. Maybe it was time to understand that things were the way they were, and my fake triathlon wasn't going to change that.

I plopped down on the sand and dipped my toes into the freezing water. I took them out and piled sand onto my feet, knowing I had a decision to make, and fast. Mom and Britta were talking behind me, and they had nice fake smiles plastered on their faces, and I was sure neither one would mind if I said I wanted to leave. In a half hour, I could be snuggled up in blankets and sweatpants, eating pancakes, all memory of this day wiped out with a boatload of bananas and chocolate chips. I could come up with some other project. One that was a little less triathlon-y.

I was just deciding to call it quits when I heard his voice.

"Let's get this party started! I am Rafael, hear me roar!" No. Way. I turned around at the sound of ripping. Rafael had been wearing a T-shirt; now he wasn't. He grinned at me, shook out his arms, and gave them each a kiss. "Yeah, you heard me. And yes, these guns did just rip the crud out of that shirt. Now let's do this!"

"Rafael Luis Garcia! That was a good shirt!" His

mom came up behind him and picked the shirt up from the ground. She waved it around like she was disgusted, but she laughed, too, and so did I. He was here! Rafael was here!

I looked behind him and saw a blurry-ish mob of people coming around the path. There was Kaya. Viv. Viv's mom. Mr. Alvarado. Ms. Wolfson. The salesgirl, Mei, from ZOOM. Tons of people from school. Seriously, tons! When I thought that was everyone, more and more came around the path. My jaw dropped so far down it practically plummeted into the freezing water and I didn't even care. What were all these people doing here? I'd only told my friends. I didn't think anyone would want to come, based on what I already knew about them, and especially based on their bubbles.

And speaking of bubbles, there were a lot of variations of the same thing over a lot of people's heads. *I hope I can do this. I hope this works out. I hope I remember how to swim. I hope I don't finish last. Hope.* Hope, hope, hope.

If they could all have that word floating above their heads, why couldn't I get some into my heart?

Suddenly I wasn't cold anymore. There was excitement in the air instead of a chill. People tore off their layers, tossing them wherever, and ran toward the water, pushing each other and laughing and finally lining up in one big, long row. I was so excited that I didn't even mind standing next to Viv Carlson.

"I can't believe there are so many people here," I said to her. "I can't believe *you* are here!"

She smiled. "I can."

I gave her a look.

"It was no big deal. I just posted online about it to my nine hundred friends and had my mom mention it at a couple spin classes. And then I had Rafael put up some posters at ZOOM and Kaya put some up at her therapist's office."

I gave her another look. Kaya, Rafael, and Viv Carlson did all that? For the race? For *me*? Before I could let that sink in, Kaya came up on my other side.

"How are you? Are you okay?" I asked. What I really wanted to know was, were *we* okay?

She nodded and stared at the water like it was going to eat her for dinner, spit her back out, and eat her again.

Scared of Stuff Kaya was here this morning, not Kaya the Adventurous Girl. That person would still take some getting used to, but Kaya liked being her. And I liked Kaya, well, however Kaya wanted to be.

"You can do it," I said.

"I can do it," she repeated, like she'd been practicing this a lot. "I will. I can. I can. I will."

"Everybody ready?" I gave Kaya a hug as everyone

clapped and cheered. "On your mark," I yelled, "get set, go!"

We splashed into the water at warp speed. Since we could only use the area marked off for swimming and not really the rest of the lake, I figured we'd all just swim in circles until we felt like we'd swum enough.

Only I didn't account for this many people. As I flopped around like an uncoordinated fish, I realized I didn't totally recognize a lot of the heads flopping around in there with me. Was that Rafael's little brother? And both of Kaya's dads? There were kids, parents, teenagers, teachers, everybody. People I didn't know. There were more people than there was water.

But I didn't have to yell at anyone to stop swimming. Some people waded over to the shallow part and sat there, waiting their turn until there was more room. Some people stood or sat on docks near where people were doing laps, waving and screaming and cheering like crazy. No one complained that someone was in the way or taking too long or doing a bad job. People just kept clapping.

Viv was the first one out of the water, but she did a weird Viv thing—instead of taking a running leap onto a bike like I thought she would, she got out of the water, toweled off, and stood there.

And then when our friend Miguel got out next, he

did the same thing. And so did Rafael and some old guy I didn't know and some kid whose teeth were chattering but whose mouth was smiling.

They waited. They waited for Rafael's mom, who splashed hard but not very fast. They waited for Mr. Alvarado, who made a lot of this-water-is-going-up-my-nose noises but kept swimming anyway. They waited for Kaya, and they waited for me.

"You did it!" I told Kaya when I got out.

"I did." She grinned. "I really did!"

When everyone was out and mostly dry, we headed over to a giant row of bikes. Mei's parents owned a bike rental company, and she'd gotten them to donate some for us to use. Only instead of the five I'd asked for, there were a whole bunch. Had Viv Carlson talked to her, too?

"Wait!" Kaya yelled louder than I'd ever heard her yell before. Everyone froze. "We forgot! Viv and I made T-shirts!"

I made a scowly face. Things had been going so well, and now she was making all of us stop and wait and watch her and Viv and Rafael put on the dumb shirts they'd made without me?

Kaya ran over to her backpack and pulled one out. It was white with a ton of designs on it in different colors.

She waved it in the direction of the group. "I have enough for everyone!"

I looked closer at the letters. It didn't say TEAM SKVR or VSKR or any of the other combinations. It said TEAM EVERYBODY.

My face broke into a grin. Now that was a team I belonged on. And even better, one I was invited to.

I ran over as fast as I could. "Is there one for me?"

"Of course." Kaya was taking them out of her backpack one after the next after the next. When I thought for sure they were gone, she'd take out another.

And there it was, my very own TEAM EVERYBODY shirt. And she really had them for everybody, even parents and teachers and Ms. Wolfson.

"Why'd you make them like this?" I pulled the shirt over my head. I was way worn-out from swimming, but at the same time, I had all the energy in the world.

"Instead of our initials? Well, Viv did invite everybody on the planet. We didn't want anyone to feel left out."

But that's exactly how you made me feel before, I wanted to say. But I didn't have time to say it, because it was time to get biking.

"Ready, set, go!" Mei did the honors this time. She waved a neon-pink headband that had been around her head and flashed me a big grin.

Okay. All I had to do was not fall off. I wasn't going to fall off. No. I was most likely, very hopefully, totally not going to fall off. Oh pancakes, I was definitely going to fall off.

I took my time and tried my hardest to concentrate on steering, not speed. I weaved my way through all the people. It almost seemed like there were more bikers than there were swimmers.

"What up, Mini Mulvaney!" BFF Britta hollered as she swerved around me. "Yeah, I know, Britta on a bike. Wheeeee!"

I looked for Mom, but she was still standing on the sidelines. At least she was watching with a little smile on her face—that was what I wanted—but my heart still dropped seeing it. Mom could totally do this race, so why wasn't she?

I grabbed on to my handlebars and clutched them for dear life. We were biking down the path along the lake for a few miles; then we'd turn around and run back to where we started. It was a major amount of distance, but it actually didn't feel too bad. In fact, with my T-shirt clinging to my body and the wind pushing me forward, it was almost kind of fun.

I didn't even mind the cold weather. In fact, it seemed like it was getting better. The black clouds had turned to gray, and the temperature had warmed up. I rounded the last corner, almost catching up to Rafael, who was having the time of his life. "Yee-haw!" he yelled. "Biking rules!"

We crossed the end of the bike trail around the same time, and we both let out loud whoops and squeals. I had actually biked that whole way without anything bad happening! My legs felt wobbly and tingled like crazy, but I wanted to keep going. I couldn't stop now.

Just like we had with swimming, we waited for everyone to finish biking, then we all tied up our helmets around the bikes and got back into position for running. No one talked; the only sounds you could hear were hearts thumping and lungs pumping. I wasn't the only one who was tired—or determined.

I was about to say *go* when I noticed one more person jogging over to join us. I squinted and looked closer. Could it be? Was it really? Holy pancakes with extra chocolate chips and an entire tree's worth of bananas. It was *my mom*. Molly Mulvaney. The Mom who knew who I was. Who knew who she was. The real Mom.

"On your mark . . ." Rafael started.

"Get set . . ." Kaya, Viv, and I chimed in.

"Go!" yelled pretty much everyone.

This was it.

We took off running. I ran so quickly—like Mom and I had when we played the townspeople game at the gym—that I forgot about everything. I didn't check to make sure Mom and Britta were still going. I didn't worry about where Kaya and Rafael were or what they were thinking about me or each other or anything. I passed dozens of people and didn't stop to check who had bubbles over their heads or if those bubbles were sad ones. I just kept running and running and running. And it felt like that day at the gym with Mom, but different. Better. It wasn't just excitement that my feet were working; it was like taking that first amazing breath of fresh air after you'd had a stuffy nose for months.

I was more than excited, really.

I was free.

And the feeling carried me so far that I didn't notice the crack of thunder—or the very large man, until he was right in front of us, waving his arms and yelling, *"Everybody freeze."*

33

THE END OF THE RACE

WE FROZE.

"You can't be here," Giant Scary Guy said, crossing his Giant Scary Guy arms. He was wearing a park uniform and a name tag that said RICK.

Kaya and I exchanged nervous glances. Since when was an outside, public place somewhere you couldn't be?

I couldn't help peeking up at the sky. It wasn't raining, but that creepy, ominous thunder was crackling, almost like it was trying to warn us that there was going to be a downpour any second.

"Why can't we be here?"

I looked around, trying to figure out whose loud, forceful voice that was.

It was LaMya's. Aka the Girl Who Wanted to Speak in Front of a Group, and Had.

Huh.

"Well, many reasons. One, any large-group athletic event needs to be approved by the department. Two, any large-group athletic events are typically on the other side of the beach." He pointed, like we had no clue where the other side would be. "Three, *that* side of the beach has a lifeguard on duty, which you must have in order to swim here. And finally, I saw you biking in an area strictly designated for walking."

Whoa. Who knew a beach had so many rules? And somehow, without trying, I'd managed to break them all.

Yup, there was rain now. Of course. It was like a combination of the worst nightmare and horror movie ever. Some people started slinking off. Others didn't even slink; they full-on ran. Didn't they care that they wouldn't finish the mini-triathlon? They were giving up? Was that it? In December 1955, there were major floods in California, but no one gave up on having Christmas. There was a huge blizzard in Minnesota on Halloween in 1991, but you can bet no one missed their trick-or-treating. But now everyone was going to bail just because of a guy and a little bit of water?

I stepped forward. "We didn't know about those rules, and we didn't break them on purpose." Raindrops pelted me on the head like they were laughing at me.

Mom put her arm around me. "Soph," she whispered.

"It doesn't matter, whatever he says. No one's racing in this. It's over."

Giant Scary Guy frowned. "I'm sorry," he said. "It's time to pack it in."

Some water trickled down my face and I had no idea if it was rain or tears. My eyeballs felt after-ten-thirty-at-night droopy. So much for my big new race. So much for reminding Mom how stuff like this could be good and fun. So much for everything.

Mom poked me in the side as more clouds opened up and rain came down. "Come on," she said. "Let's go."

She linked her arm through mine and sort of dragged me toward the parking lot. We jogged. As the rain came down harder and faster, our jog changed to a run. And then our run turned into a run-as-fast-as-you-possibly-can dash, and so did everyone else's.

And something about it wasn't so awful at all.

I linked my free arm through Ms. Wolfson's. She linked hers through Kaya's, who linked hers through Rafael's, and so on until my group of triathlon people was mostly in one long chain, running through the rain together.

"This is ridiculous!" I yelled, opening my mouth to catch some huge droplets.

"This is everything," Mom yelled back. "Wolfson women are not doormats!"

As the parking lot came into view, everyone let out a huge cheer.

"It's the finish line!" Rafael yelled.

"Run!" Kaya hollered.

"It's the finish line!" Ms. Wolfson repeated, louder.

"We're running!" Mom yelled. Glancing over at her, I couldn't tell if the water in her eyes was rain or tears, either.

There were bubbles over people's heads—some happy, some sad, some a little bit of both—but I kept looking forward. I didn't have to stop and know and help right this second. I could just . . . keep my eyes on my own cards, sometimes. I could just keep going.

A second later, we all crossed the parking lot line together. There weren't ribbons or balloons or a giant scoreboard with our times like there would have been in the real thing, but there was a lot of laughter and hugging and falling over in a fun way, not a getting-hurt way. We hadn't actually successfully finished the mini-triathlon, but something about it felt exactly like we had. All of us. Together. It wasn't about crossing a finish line or being the best or solving everybody's problems perfectly. It was about doing your best, and having people to race with.

34
NEWS

MY CERTIFICATES WERE SERIOUSLY SOGGY. I GUESS THAT'S what I got for taking them out before the race. You couldn't see the border of stars I'd hand-drawn on each and every one, or "Triathlon" in really fancy writing, or the clip-art gold medals I'd printed and glued on. Also, there definitely weren't enough for everybody.

It didn't matter. A few of us held them up and posed for a picture right there in the rainy parking lot. Of course, the rain had gone from pouring like crazy to a teeny little drizzle by the time we got there, but it didn't matter; we were already soaked. And I kinda wouldn't have wanted it any other way.

A giant white van pulled into the parking lot right as we came apart after the picture. Mom's face went from happy to confused in two seconds flat.

Two guys got out of the van. One was holding a ginormous video camera.

"Molly?"

"Blake? Shel? What are you doing here?"

"My buddy Rick from Beach Services called to say there were a bunch of loonies running around in the rain. Thought I'd come take a look. Slow news day."

Mom and I shared a look that said, "Wait, who is he calling a looney?" and also, "Slow news day? Uhhh, hello? We have news!"

My grin got even bigger. Mom and I were sharing looks.

"Well, there actually was a triathlon here this morning." Mr. Alvarado stepped forward. "Sophie organized one since there was a problem with the one she and her friends had intended to do. They were doing it for their risk project for my class." He looked really proud.

"Is that so? You didn't give me a heads-up, Mol." Blake swatted Mom playfully on the wrist. Ohhh, so that's who Blake was. I knew his name sounded familiar. He was the guy they hired after they banished Mom to our couch.

"Ha. I didn't know what it'd be like until now."

"Well . . ." Blake looked my way. "Sophie, I know it's kind of short notice, but we've got a three-minute human interest segment that needs filling, and it sounds like you had quite the adventure here. Feel like sharing with, oh, ten million people or so?"

I gulped. I'd hoped to be on TV. This was what I wanted. But now that the bright light of the camera was blinding me and Blake was looking at me like I was really, really important, being on TV seemed scarier than taking a ride on the *Mayflower* in 1620.

"Do it, Sophie!" Kaya elbowed me. "An Adventurous Girl would."

"Yep," Rafael agreed. "Come on! You can be almost as famous as me. I ripped my shirt off at the start of our race, thus I am awesome," he explained to Blake. "I'd be happy to share that with your viewers. Also, do you have any connections at ZOOM Athletics? Specifically, their Very Warm Glove Department?"

I shoved him out of the way.

"Okay," I said. "I'll do it."

"That's the spirit. Okay, we only have a few minutes, so I'll need to pin this microphone to your shirt, and, oh, I need your mom to sign this waiver." He grabbed a clipboard from his backseat and handed it to Mom. "Anything you need before we film?" He reached back into the van and rummaged through a duffel bag. "I have water, a granola bar, uh . . . water or a granola bar?"

"Well, there is one thing I want," I said. Then I leaned in and whispered it in his ear.

"Sure, we can do that," he said. "Not a problem at all."

Ms. Wolfson flashed me a thumbs-up sign, and Blake did, too, and before I knew it, the camera was rolling, the lights were flashing, and I was on TV.

35
FIGURING IT OUT

"WE'RE COMING TO YOU LIVE FROM BRIDGEMONT BEACH," Blake said, "where, despite rules, regulations, and the biggest downpour we've had in over five years, twelve-year-old Sophie Mulvaney planned and implemented her own mini-triathlon. Sophie, what inspired you to do this?"

I blinked a billion times. *Words,* I thought. *Say words.*

"Well, I needed to do a risk project for school," I said. "And my friends and I were going to do a mini-triathlon, because it was pretty scary for all of us for different reasons. I forgot to turn in our registration forms, and I felt really bad. And I still really wanted to do the race. Or *a* race."

"Looks like you weren't the only one," said Blake. "How'd you get such a huge turnout?"

"My friends did that." I shot them all a huge grin, and they grinned back.

"And I noticed that your mom did the race with you as well," Blake said. "Folks, you might recognize Molly Mulvaney. She used to be a broadcaster here on Channel 23. Molly, can you tell us why you supported Sophie's idea, and why you ran the race yourself?"

Mom stepped forward and swept her bangs to the side.

"I, uh . . ." She stared at the camera. Then she blinked and suddenly looked like her old self. Mom stood up straight and gave the camera a big smile. "I used to be a big runner," she said. "Really into races. I did a ton of them, and then I stopped. Sophie motivated me to get back into it, to do what I used to love, even if it was hard, even if it scared me." Mom laughed. "Sophie's a better adult than I am. Do you run, Blake?"

I grinned. This was one of Mom's old techniques. She'd report on something and then totally surprise whoever else was around by asking if they'd ever tried whatever she was talking about, and then she'd make them do it. It made for some pretty hilarious TV.

Blake laughed. "Not at all."

Mom pointed to where we had come from.

"Then you better get going," she said. "But watch out for Rick, the guy on beach patrol. Viewers, it turns out there are rules on beaches. More on that later." She nudged Blake. "The people are waiting," she said. Blake looked at me and I shrugged. *Sorry,* I mouthed. Blake chuckled, and he took off toward the water in his shiny black shoes and dress pants. He slogged along *really* slowly. Before we ran together in the gym, Mom hadn't been running since her last race. But it looked like Blake hadn't been running ever.

"Folks, this has been Blake Taylor and Molly Mulvaney from Channel 23, saying go run somewhere today with someone you love. Don't forget to tune in live at ten for more happy news. And, you know, the rest of the news, too." Mom grinned and the camera guy pressed a button and gave her a hand signal. "All clear," he said, and put the camera down. Mom rushed up and gave him a hug. "Missed you, Shel," she said.

Then she turned to me and hugged me so hard that my feet almost lifted right up off the ground. Her cheeks were glowing. All of her was glowing, really.

"This day," she said, "has been the best."

"Totally," I agreed.

Even though our race and our TV appearance were done, people lingered in the parking lot like it was the place to party. A lot of people came up to me to say good job and congratulations. Some of those people were my friends, and some I didn't know. And almost all of them had that same glow that Mom did.

Except for one.

"What's wrong?" I asked. Kaya sat all by herself on the curb with her head in her hands. She looked up at me with tears in her eyes.

"Nothing. It's dumb. I should be happy. I swam!"

"You totally swam," I said. "You swam seriously fast, too. You could probably beat a lifeguard in a race. Or a shark!"

She giggled. "Right. It's just—I dunno, it's everything."

"I'm so sorry we couldn't do the real triathlon," I told her.

"I know you are. Rafael knows, too. That's why we made you our new project!"

"Your . . . huh?"

"We told Mr. Alvarado some new project ideas, but he kept asking about the triathlon, so we told him how we couldn't do it anymore because of you. And he told us that sometimes friendship is a risk. Like a real grown-up mature friendship, where you forgive people when they make mistakes instead of just not talking to them anymore or whatever. It's hard and scary, sometimes. He said it would be cool—and risky—if we supported you even though we were still a little mad. After all, you were making a whole new race, like, *for us*."

I smiled. I'd never thought of friendship as risky before, but maybe it kinda was.

"And, as your supportive friend, I have to tell you that what you said to me about Rafael liking Viv really bugged me, and I can't forget about it no matter what."

"Because you're going out with him?"

"What?" She gave me a funny look. "No, but I kinda like him as more than a friend. Or I think I do, at least." Her face turned bright pink. "Sometimes I call him my boyfriend in my head. Super embarrassing, right?"

She called him her boyfriend in her head?

They weren't really going out?

That bubble . . . was a *lie*?

But it was what she was thinking!

I had been sure that Kaya's bubble was a fact. It seemed as obvious as how popular William Seward must have been after he bought Alaska for the United States.

I guess it sorta *was* a fact, though—it was real to her, even if it wasn't, like, real real.

Which maybe I could have figured out if I had talked to her about it before now.

"I don't think he likes Viv," I told Kaya.

"You don't?" Her eyes got all big and hopeful.

"No. I know I said that, but I was wrong. I lied, and I'm sorry. But the thing is, I think I might kinda like him, too." Our eyes locked. "But maybe not. I'm not sure. I've only ever really liked Demarius."

"Maybe I'm not sure, either," Kaya said, looking out into the parking lot. Rafael was dancing with Mr. Alvarado's kids. "He's just so fun. And I think it would be cool to go out with someone."

"Sophie, Kaya!" Mom hollered, and waved her arms. Everyone was getting into cars. "Come on! Celebration pancake party!"

Pancake party! Heck to the yes! I grabbed Kaya's hand and pulled her up.

"We'll figure this out later," I promised. "But right now, we need to eat pancakes."

"With extra chocolate chips," she said.

"Definitely."

36

PANCAKE PARTY

OUR GROUP TOOK UP FIVE BIG TABLES AT THE DINER. I felt kinda bad for the other people who were there when we barged in, but they seemed okay when they realized we were the people from TV. Plus Kaya had a few extra TEAM EVERYBODY shirts, so she gave some out to strangers.

No one stayed in their seats once we all sat down. Everybody bopped around from table to table. Viv, especially, couldn't sit still. One second she was with her mom, then she was with Rafael, then Mr. Alvarado, then Mei. Everybody. Even when the food came, she bounced around. But that's how she'd always been at school—popular, floating from group to group—and that's how she was at the pancake place.

And that's when I understood something major, and

I didn't need a bubble to do it. Friendship could be risky. For everyone. Even Viv Carlson.

I went and sat by her.

"Hello?" she said, like it was a question.

"Hello," I said. "Can I ask you something?"

"I guess?"

"Before you started hanging out with Kaya and Rafael all the time, who were your friends?"

Viv squirmed around in her seat.

"What do you mean? A lot of people. Everybody, basically. The group from dance team, the people at the gym, the cast of the musical, everyone online . . ."

"Yeah, but, like, who'd you hang out with the most? Who knew you the best?"

She opened her mouth, then closed it, then looked me right in the eye. "Can I tell you the truth about something?"

"The truth would be great."

"When I said my risk project was something more challenging than a triathlon? Well, you guys were my project. Being part of, like, a real group of friends. I mean, I'm kinda friends with everybody, but nobody really knows me that well. And I don't really hang out with anyone outside of school or my activities. So my goal was to, you know, really be part of something. Your something. You and Rafael and Kaya. I like you guys a lot."

I looked away. This whole time, her big, secret, "more challenging" project . . . was being our friend. And not just being Rafael and Kaya's friend. She wanted to be my friend, too.

"I, um"—she was practically whispering—"I feel weird about myself, sometimes. Like I'm all awkward and not cool enough to have real friends and stuff. It's really embarrassing, but sometimes I tell myself in my head how great I am. Maybe someday I'll actually believe it. Hanging out with you guys makes me feel like I actually am great."

"But it seemed like you didn't want to hang out with me. You only ever wanted to hang out with Kaya and Rafael."

"Are you kidding?"

"No?"

"I wanted to hang out with you the most. You're the coolest person ever. I was nervous you wouldn't like me. I thought if I could be friends with Kaya and Rafael first, and they liked me, then maybe you'd like me, too."

So she wasn't plotting anything weird or evil. She was plotting *friendship*. With *me*! And I hadn't noticed, because I was so stuck on thinking of her as the person

I thought she was and thinking about her bubbles in the way I wanted to think about them.

"That's a really cool project," I told her.

"Thanks." She turned her attention back to her strawberry pancake and took a bite. "Hey," she added. "You were telling the truth, weren't you? In fourth grade. You put that sign on my locker. I always kinda knew it." She smiled, but scooted her chair back like she was going to get up.

"Hey, wait," I said. "Stay. Let's hang out."

And we did.

And you know what?

Hanging out with Viv Carlson was actually pretty fun.

37

ALL THE TRUTH

THAT AFTERNOON, AFTER THE PANCAKE PARTY, I ASKED Mom to take me to the public library so I could do some history research. The thing was, what if everything I thought I knew I actually didn't? What if I'd sped through things I'd read, or heard wrong on the History Channel, or twisted and turned things in my brain so they sounded like facts I thought were cool to hear?

It was time to find the truth. All the truth. Even if I didn't like it.

The first thing I did, with the super cool librarian's help, was look up some information about Alaska. That was one thing I always thought was awesome. This guy, William Seward, was just a regular dude, but he made such a huge difference. I'd never been to Alaska, but I couldn't imagine the United States without it.

Only, as I looked up more and more information, some articles were called "Alaska Purchase," but others were called "Seward's Folly." As it turned out, a lot of people thought it was dumb to buy Alaska. They thought it was a mistake. They made fun of him. He was famous, but not everybody loved him. Not even close.

I kept researching. Walter Washington Williams, the 117-year-old last remaining veteran of the Civil War, may have been a total faker. According to some articles, there was no evidence that he had ever served in the war, or that he was ever 117.

More searches for more topics came back with all kinds of results. People had tons of opinions about the best kings and queens and presidents and every other kind of leader and place and event there ever was.

Sure, you couldn't really argue with dates and places and stuff, but besides those things, there weren't any clear answers anywhere.

Maybe there weren't clear answers with people I knew, either.

Maybe not even the facts were facts.

I had liked history because it had always been something I could depend on. It didn't go from adventurous to not adventurous or from happy to sad or anything else. It didn't break up with you or fire you or leave you out. It seemed like it was just there, being all fact-y and honest and cool. Now, I realized that I might never know the full truth. Not about history, and not about anybody's thoughts.

But maybe I didn't need history to depend on anymore. I had people I could depend on. And they could depend on me. And it didn't matter whether we made mistakes or felt sad or lied to ourselves about having a boyfriend when we didn't. We'd be there for each other no matter what. I *did* want to be that person Ms. Wolfson said I was, the person Mom could be her real self around, even if that self was sad sometimes.

No matter what, I had people I could count on, and they could count on me. And that was the best fact of all.

38

THE END OF THE BUBBLES

"I KNOW WHAT HAPPENED TO THE QUEEN," I TOLD
Dr. Llama when I saw him a couple weeks after the race.

"Oh?"

"Well, I mean, I don't really. But I have a guess. I think she was scared when the war was upon her. Not just for herself, but for her whole kingdom. She felt like it was her job to protect everybody from it, since she sorta brought it on herself, even though she didn't know exactly why or how." I leaned forward in my chair. "We don't know if the war really was her fault, but maybe that's not even the point. Whether it was or not, she felt like it was her job to fix it, because she was the queen and she knew so much about her people and cared about them and wanted to make their problem go away.

So she tried to fix it all by herself, over and over and over again."

"And?"

"And that was nice of her, but it didn't really work. She was so worried about her people that their worries became her worries. But she didn't even bother asking them if they were freaked out by the war or if they had ideas to stop it. She did what she thought she should do, but not what people actually needed."

"What did they need?"

I leaned back in the brown chair. It was so comfy. I didn't know why I used to hate it so much.

"A friend," I said.

Dr. Llama smiled. "So you think the war turned out okay?"

"I think once the queen asked her friends, *Hey, what do you guys think we should do? Are you scared?* and actually listened to what they said, then yeah. I think it turned out okay. Because even if they lost the war, they still had each other."

He didn't say anything, just looked at me with that same glowy face I saw on so many people after the triathlon.

"The queen asking her friends for their ideas reminds me of what you did with your race," he said. "You took some responsibility off yourself and gave people a way to help themselves. It's wonderful to want to help people, Sophie," he said. "As long as you can do it without feeling guilty for their problems. Sometimes it's no one person's fault when there's a war. Or a bubble. Or a friendship struggle or a parent's sadness or anything else." He shrugged his giant shoulders. "Sometimes war just comes."

I nodded.

"So, have you seen any new bubbles lately?"

"None." They'd disappeared after the triathlon. "They're totally gone."

"Maybe you don't need them anymore."

Yeah. I smiled a little to myself. Something about that sounded exactly right.

But something about it sounded a little wrong, too.

"Does that mean I don't need you anymore?" I asked. My problem was solved, which was good news. So why did I feel like I was about to get kicked out of the history museum before I'd gotten a chance to see everything?

Dr. Llama smiled. "You can come back anytime you want, Sophie. I'll always be here for you. Therapy isn't just about solving problems. It's about listening, talking, growing. Becoming the best version of you that you can be and finding your place in the big world. There's always more to learn if you're willing to do the work."

I smiled back. Maybe I wasn't always up for doing the work—after all, I did have homework to do and friends to hang out with—but it was good to know that he would always be here if I needed him.

"You know," I added, "it turned out that some of the bubbles weren't the whole truth. I had all the facts, but they weren't facts at all."

"Oh?"

"Yeah. I was so sure that things were a certain way, but I was wrong. I heard the words in people's heads, but I didn't really, like, ask anybody if they were true. Does that make any sense?"

He nodded. "And even if you ask people if they're true, they might not be honest with you. You may never know anyone's full truth. But if you do your part, and listen thoughtfully and show that you're trustworthy, you might be surprised at how much people open up." He paused. "You know how I always ask how you are? And then don't say anything?"

"Yeah?"

"It's because I know if I wait long enough, if I listen, you'll always tell me."

He was right. I always did.

There was one more thing I needed to know.

"You believe me that I really saw the bubbles, right?"

"I believe experience shapes who you are, and I'd never question your experience."

I'd take that as a yes.

39

AN ADVENTURE

BFF BRITTA PICKED ME UP FROM DR. LLAMA'S BECAUSE
something had come up for Mom. When we got home,
I heard laughter coming out of the stairs. Mom's laughter. And a guy's laughter, too.

My heart sank right through the floor and into the
basement. Noooo. Problem one: Mom was in the stairs,
and we didn't take the stairs anymore, ever. Problem
two: a guy's laughter. All I could think was Pratik. And
everything we'd been through disappearing right before
my eyes. I pictured Mom starting this all over. Getting
back together with Pratik. Being upset because of Pratik not being a good boyfriend. Breaking up with Pratik.
Staring at stuff. Imaginary locks.

I knew none of it was my fault, but I couldn't let it
happen. This wasn't only about Mom being happy or

sad. Maybe it was a little about me being happy or sad, too. I didn't want Pratik back anymore. I wanted someone who'd run with us, who'd stick by us when things got tough. And while it'd be cool to have a dad-like person someday, right now I just needed my mom.

The door to the stairway opened.

"No!" I yelled at the top of my lungs. Mom stared at me with a very worried look on her face. So did the guy she was with. Hey, that guy looked familiar. "Blake?"

"Hey, Sophie!"

"What's, uh, what's going on here, exactly?" I asked.

"Oh, I was just walking Blake out," Mom said, like it was obvious. She had a huge smile on her face. That wasn't good, either. Was Blake her new boyfriend?

"I was chatting with your mom about that condo that's for sale next door," he said. "I've always loved this neighborhood."

Oh, no. Well, that was worse. My mind raced, thinking of everything that could go wrong when Mom and Blake broke up. Forget not being able to walk down the stairs—with Blake next door, I wouldn't be allowed to walk down our street. I'd have to take the long way, like, everywhere. Walking to school would take an extra twenty minutes, which meant I'd have to wake up twenty minutes earlier every day. And even as a morning person, twenty minutes earlier was not going to work for me.

"Are you sure that's a good idea?" I eyed Mom. I was talking to Blake, yeah, but I was really talking to her.

"Definitely," he said. "Puts me much closer to my gym and my new personal trainer." He winked at Mom.

"Wait, what?"

"I'll leave you two to chat about what a pathetic runner I am," Blake joked. "I'll see you next week, Molly."

"Sounds good! Bring better shoes than the ones you wore to the beach."

Blake waved, and then he was gone.

I turned to Mom.

"What just happened?"

She laughed. "Surprise! I got a job as a trainer at the gym."

"But . . . what about Channel 23?"

Mom wrinkled her nose. "I don't want to work there," she said. "Working in TV wasn't quite right for me, and neither was working at home." She shrugged. "I guess I'm still figuring out what I want to be when I grow up."

I looked at the floor. I knew now that things weren't always one person's fault, but it still seemed like I had an awful lot to do with Mom losing her job in the first place. "If I hadn't made you lose your job, you wouldn't still have to figure it out. I'm sorry."

"Soph . . ." Mom grabbed my chin and lifted my face up so it was even with hers. "What are you talking about? I *quit* my job at Channel 23. I mean, yeah, things weren't going great, but it was only because my heart wasn't in it. I was good at it, sure. Still am. In fact, they asked me to come back, and I thought about it, but I turned them down. Reporting didn't make me feel the way I did when I was running with you at the gym and during the race, like I was strong and in control. I want to help other people feel that way. It's nobody's fault that my news job didn't work out. Especially not yours."

I let out a giant breath I hadn't realized I'd been holding. It was nobody's fault. Especially not mine. And now Mom had a new job that might really make her happy . . . and I'd sorta helped her find it. Which was kinda awesome.

"But you were so sad when you got home from the meeting with your boss," I said. "I thought you got fired."

Mom's face changed. "I'm so sorry you thought that," she said. "I guess I just assumed you knew, or something. I should have told you."

"Yeah, you should have," I said. "You were so sad. You've been so sad all the time!"

"I know. The truth is, Soph, sometimes I get really sad like this. It's something I've been dealing with for a lot of my life. I usually don't let you see it, but this time,

I don't know . . . I just didn't have the energy to call someone."

"Call someone like who?"

"Like Ms. Wolfson, usually."

I raised my eyebrows. Those weren't just fun sleepovers because Mom was busy? They were because she was sad?

"You've really inspired me, though," Mom said, tickling my arm. "Going to your Dr. Llama guy. I used to go to someone like that, but I stopped when it got hard. It's a lot easier to stay quiet. I think I'm going to go back. You've been really brave, Soph. I'm glad those bubbles finally went away."

I smiled, but something was still bugging me.

"Are you going to go out with Blake now?"

"What? No way." Mom laughed. "He's married. But even if he wasn't, I wouldn't date him. Single Blake wouldn't be right for me, even though he's cute." She giggled. "I know that deep down. I'm going to start listening to what I know deep down. And I'm going to stop being a doormat. And hey, maybe we should take that stuff out of the box in the cabinet and hang it up again. Those race numbers and stuff. I've done some pretty cool things, you know?"

I didn't say anything. Instead, I hugged her. In the lobby. For a super long time. And Mom didn't pull away or realize we were downstairs and we needed not to be. A thousand Pratiks could have walked by and we wouldn't have cared. In fact, when Pratik actually did walk by, Mom didn't even flinch, and neither did I.

"Want to go have an adventure?" she asked.

"I think we just did," I said.

40

CLIMBING MOUNT FITZ ROY

"MAYBE WE COULD DO ROCK PAPER SCISSORS?"

"There's gotta be some kind of mathematical equation that will calculate who he's more compatible with."

"Then what is it?"

"I dunno."

"But you're the math expert."

She shrugged at me like, *Well then, we really have a problem, don't we?*

Kaya and I were sitting on the floor, slumped against her locker, trying to figure out the Rafael business. We were purposely avoiding Our Spot until we had reached some kind of decision, which was turning out to be way harder than we'd thought.

"Look what I got!" Rafael zoomed down the hall waving his hands in everybody's faces. Along with his jeans

and T-shirt, he was wearing these massive gray gloves that made him look like a fuzzy robot. It was pretty cool—after my interview had been on TV, ZOOM Athletics called and apologized for not letting us into the race, even though it wasn't really their fault. They even offered gift cards for all four of us.

Kaya and I looked at each other and burst out laughing.

"You know, maybe you can have him," I said. "It's okay with me. I still don't know if I even like him or just liked that I thought he liked me."

I looked at him. Did he like me? I might never really know. Right now, it seemed like he liked the gloves more than anything or anyone else.

"No, it's okay. You can go out with him. I'll be fine," Kaya said.

We started laughing again as Rafael swung back around the hall and shoved his hands in people's faces some more. As he got closer to us, my heart didn't pound one bit, and I felt weirdly super relieved by that. Kaya and I were back, and right now, that was what mattered most.

"Hey, don't you wonder what happened with me and those bubbles?" I asked her.

"Uh, yeah! You never really told me anything!"

"You never really asked!"

We looked at each other and exploded with laughs a third time.

"Let's do better at that," I said. "Asking each other stuff. And telling. Okay?"

"For sure," she agreed. "So are things okay with the bubbles now? Did you figure out what the deal was?"

"Yeah," I said. "I went to a therapist. He helped me, but mostly he helped me figure it out myself."

"Therapists are annoyingly cool like that," she said.

"Seriously."

"Isn't it weird that we're the only people in school who have seen them, but we never talk about it?"

I nodded. "I was embarrassed at first. It felt like an embarrassing thing."

"Yeah, I get that. But it shouldn't be. I liked going to mine. Did you like yours?"

"A lot."

We sat quietly, looking up at all the people walking by. Maybe we were the only kids in our school who had gone to therapists, but I had a feeling that wasn't even close to being a fact.

. . .

With only a minute to go till the bell rang, Kaya left to talk to a teacher and Rafael rushed up to me, gloves out. Some people think gloves were first invented by the Greeks. Others think it was the Romans. And since gloves weren't really popular till Queen Elizabeth I wore them, some people think the invention was hers. I wasn't exactly sure where I stood on that historical tidbit, but I knew that gloves sure made Rafael happy, and that was pretty great.

"Have you had a chance to see the amazingness up close yet? Look!" He shoved his hands in my face.

I laughed. "Nice. Hey, Rafael?"

He stopped moving for a second and put his hands down by his sides. "Yeah?"

"I just wanted to say thanks, for getting me to do the triathlon and stuff. You were right that I wasn't acting like myself. There was some . . . stuff going on."

"What kind of stuff?"

"Well . . . just, I was sorta mad at myself for some things that weren't actually my fault. And then I started seeing these weird bubbles over people's heads that said what they were thinking. Basically my world kinda went bonkers."

I held my breath and waited for him to make some kind of joke or start talking about his gloves again, but he didn't. Instead, he put one of his fuzzy hands on my shoulder.

"That must have been tough," he said.

"Uh, yeah. It was," I said.

"You could've told me."

"I know."

I did know. I knew now, at least. What had I been so afraid of? That he'd think I was weird? But if the guy you have a crush on—or even just a regular guy you're friends with—says you're weird when you tell him something important, maybe he's not that great of a friend-and/or-possible-future-boyfriend person. But Rafael was a good friend. He really, really was.

The bell rang, and Rafael and I smiled at each other as we went our different directions.

It was scary, talking to people about big-time important stuff. But sometimes, when you did, it made you feel like your friendship had just climbed a volcano as big as Mount Fitz Roy, and it was looking down at your old friendship, which was as small as a drop of water in the ocean. But now your friendship was big. Real. Powerful.

My friends and me? We were on top of the volcano, on top of the world. Together.

41
WHAT YOU DO

NOW THAT MOM WAS COOL WITH NOT HIDING IN OUR condo, she actually came with me when I hung out with Ms. Wolfson. We taught her to play cribbage, too, and it turned out that she wasn't half bad.

Mom went into the kitchen to make herself a cocoa refill, and I looked at Ms. Wolfson. This was my chance.

"Did you know about the bubbles?" I asked her. "Could you see them, too?"

"The bubbles?"

"You know. The things that said what people are thinking. Like that guy at the diner and how he was hungry." I searched her face for a sign of understanding, for a wink, for something, but I didn't see anything different.

"No," Ms. Wolfson said. "I don't see any bubbles. I'm just good at seeing people, like you are."

"Oh." I folded my hands in my lap. "But you're always so calm."

She laughed.

"Well, there's a difference between caring about someone and letting their problems be your problems. It's great to help, but you have to draw a line."

I thought of running into Ms. Wolfson that night I snuck out, coming back from her walk with her flashlight.

"You have to stay a little bit in the dark," I said.

"Exactly."

Maybe it was okay not to know what everybody was thinking all the time. Or to know, but not to let it be your entire life. It was okay to go for quick walks in the dark. To run until I felt that nice free feeling.

We sat silently, sipping our cocoa.

Ms. Wolfson said, "You know, if you want to know what someone is really thinking, there's a much simpler way."

I leaned in really close to her.

"Let me guess," I said.

She smiled and leaned in, too.

"Ask them. And listen to what they say."

"That's what you do," she said. Then Mom came back, and we all finished our cocoa, mini-marshmallows included, and played another game of cribbage.

42

THE RISKS I TOOK

I MET UP WITH KAYA, RAFAEL, AND VIV AT OUR SPOT after class the next day, but we didn't get to talk too much. Other people kept coming up to say hi. Everybody still wanted to talk about the triathlon and how cool it was.

When the bell rang and it was time to get to our next classes, I grabbed Kaya by the sleeve.

"Wait," I said. "I just wanted to see, like, how are you?"

"Good," she said, grabbing a chunk of hair. "How are you?"

"No," I said. "How *are* you?"

Her eyes widened and she bit her lip, but then her whole body relaxed. "Honestly, I'm kinda worried about our science test later. Animal cells have so many parts! How are we supposed to remember them all?"

"I know!" I said. "I'm nervous about it, too."

And even though we were worried, we smiled.

. . .

I held my breath and clenched my sweaty hands. I needed to relax. This was only a grade, and I was going to do well. Mr. Alvarado had been there. He'd worn the T-shirt, eaten the pancakes. I'd get a good grade. I had to.

"Great job, everyone," he said when he'd handed out the last paper and gone back up to the front of the room. "I am so impressed with the risks you took, the bravery you demonstrated. I am truly honored to be your teacher."

I didn't need a bubble to know that he meant it.

"All right, go ahead," he said.

"A!" LaMya shouted, then slapped a hand over her mouth. She was becoming quite a chatterbox.

"A!" Miguel shouted, too. "But our business stank," he said.

"Don't remind him," Harrison hissed.

"It was never about the success," Mr. Alvarado said. "I'm sorry I exaggerated the truth a little there. I just wanted to give you extra motivation to try your best. It was always about the try, guys. And try you did."

I inhaled and flipped mine over. *Tri* I did.

In purple marker, there was a big, fat A+. And a note.

Dear Sophie,

Congratulations on a wonderful triathlon! I applaud your effort, determination, and creativity. Not only did you challenge yourself to train for an intense athletic event, you encouraged others around you to do the same, and you took matters into your own hands in the face of extra challenges you didn't count on.

Moreover, I have a feeling the risks you've taken are far greater than running a race—that you've also faced other challenges, and taken the risks you needed to in order to tackle them head-on and come out on the other side. Well done!

I grinned and looked over at Kaya and Viv. They were smiling, too.

I thought about what Mr. Alvarado had written. He was right. Yeah, my official project was all the triathlon-y stuff, but I'd taken way more risks than I'd written about in my paper. I went to a therapist and talked about it with my friend. I had an honest conversation with Viv. I helped Mom get out of her funk—the one I didn't actually cause. I helped *me* get out of my funk. I realized that friends didn't only have to be the people you went to school with—they could be your nice neighbor with the cocoa, a high school girl who seemed snotty but actually wasn't, anybody.

Everybody.

And I did it all, even with that big worry in the back of my mind that it wouldn't work, that I'd be sad, that my future bubbles would say the same sad things as everyone else's. But maybe a sad bubble or sad thought every so often didn't mean a sad life.

There probably would be some sad things in my future. But there would be good things, too. And as long as I had my friends and family with me, and really listened to them, and we worked together, I'd never have to deal with any of those things alone. We'd cross finish lines together. And when the lines disappeared or got taken away by a big guy named Rick, we'd make it work. We'd eat pancakes and move on. Adventurous Girls did. And that was a fact.

ACKNOWLEDGMENTS

IF YOU WANT TO KNOW WHAT I'M REALLY THINKING, HERE it is: I'm the luckiest writer ever. I feel so fortunate to have been able to work on this book with a great team by my side. Thank you to Rebecca Sherman, Susan Dobinick, and Margaret Ferguson for your endless encouragement, invaluable insight, and overall amazingness.

Thank you also to Morgan Dubin, Joy Peskin, Andrea Morrison, Beth Clark, Jennifer Sale, and Karen Ninnis.

I am also thinking that the Sweet 16s, MG Beta Readers, and the Guild are the absolute best. Thanks all for your continued friendship and support.

Other people who are the best: my wonderful early readers and friends, Kalvin Nguyen, Erika David, Gail Nall, Jo Marie Bankston, and Victoria Coe. You all really helped make the story shine, as did Noah Priluck (thanks for the history tidbits!) and Francis Keating (thanks for letting me borrow the story about the queen!).

To my wonderful family and friends: AJ, Rena, Andie, Devorah, Gail, and Jess, thank you for being awesome. And of course, to my parents, Kathy and David, who started championing my books in elementary school and haven't stopped since—thank you. I have the best, most unconditional support system with you two, and am so lucky to be your daughter.

When I wrote this book, I never could have imagined that I'd find someone who would always be able to tell what I was thinking, no magical bubbles needed. Michael, not only do you know my thoughts, you know exactly how to respond to each one (usually with a combination of patience, humor, encouragement, and grilled cheese sandwiches, plus a whole lot of love). You're the best.